"Cole? What's the matter?"

"Ginny, this is...this is your first time."

"Yes. I know."

He slipped away from her. "I feel like somehow I've pushed you into this."

She couldn't believe it. Was this Cole McCallum talking? Where was the cockiness, the self-assuredness, the arrogant overconfidence she'd come to know so well?

"Cole, I want this. I want *you*. Don't you know that?"

"You say that now, but are you sure?"

She wrapped her arms around his neck. "Just kiss me."

After a moment of hesitation, he lowered his mouth to hers in a soft, gentle kiss. Ginny wanted more. *Much* more.

She grabbed his shirt, and pulled him down to her. It was a kiss so hot and wild and intense that Cole couldn't do anything but go along for the ride. Finally she pulled away, still gripping his shirt.

"Ginny? Are you trying to tell me something?"

"Yes, damn it! What am I going to have to do to convince you? Rip your clothes off? Rip my clothes off?"

Cole blinked with surprise. Then a smile spread slowly across his face. "Can I have both?"

Dear Reader,

Do you remember the girl in your high school class who didn't talk much, who was smart but socially inept, the one who the boys didn't even know existed? Do you remember the boy with the streetwise attitude who was sexy as sin, who drove the teachers crazy at the same time he made the girls swoon? What if these two people were to meet again ten years later and sparks suddenly flew?

As a writer, nothing is more fun to me than to put a hero and a heroine together who are complete opposites, then watch the fireworks. On the surface, it seems as if Cole McCallum and Ginny White are the most unlikely couple ever to share a kiss. But looks can be deceiving. Is it possible that the good girl and the bad boy are perfect for each other?

I had a wonderful time writing my first Harlequin Temptation novel, and I hope you enjoy it. Visit my Web site at www.janesullivan.com, or write me at jane@janesullivan.com. I'd love to hear from you!

Best regards,

Jane Sullivan

Books by Jane Sullivan

HARLEQUIN DUETS
33—STRAY HEARTS
48—THE MATCHMAKER'S MISTAKE

ONE HOT TEXAN
Jane Sullivan

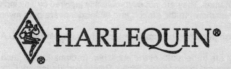

HARLEQUIN®

TORONTO • NEW YORK • LONDON
AMSTERDAM • PARIS • SYDNEY • HAMBURG
STOCKHOLM • ATHENS • TOKYO • MILAN • MADRID
PRAGUE • WARSAW • BUDAPEST • AUCKLAND

To Mom and Dad,
who always believed I could do it.

ISBN 0-373-25954-9

ONE HOT TEXAN

Copyright © 2001 by Jane Graves.

This edition published by arrangement with Harlequin Books S.A.

® and TM are trademarks of the publisher. Trademarks indicated with
® are registered in the United States Patent and Trademark Office, the
Canadian Trade Marks Office and in other countries.

Visit us at www.eHarlequin.com

Printed in U.S.A.

1

THE CLOSER Cole McCallum came to the city limits of Cold-water, Texas, the more he wanted to swing his classic Porsche around in a tire-squealing one-eighty and head back to Dallas where he belonged. He thought he'd seen the last of this god-forsaken place, only to have fate step up and slap him in the face one more time.

His first introduction to Coldwater had been eleven years ago, when he'd been forced to leave Dallas and come here for his senior year of high school. His father had been thrown in jail for writing one too many hot checks, and his mother hadn't been around since he was seven years old, so a family court judge had ordered his custody turned over to a grand-mother he barely knew. He arrived with a chip on his shoul-der the size of a concrete block. Throw in a pair of skintight jeans, a black leather jacket and a go-to-hell attitude, and the uptight citizens of Coldwater had naturally assumed he was the root of all evil. He didn't let them down.

Out of pure mischief, he committed a few minor infractions around school during his first few weeks, then dated a few of the more kiss-and-tell girls. Gossip took care of the rest. For the next year he got blamed for everything from graffiti on the water tower to Angela Putnam's period being late. And he didn't care enough to try to set anyone straight. Only his grandmother had known better, but even her reputation hadn't been able to salvage his. With the exception of the girls who swooned at his bad-boy image, the townspeople would have voted him most likely to turn up on a post-office wall. And that's why, at eighteen, he'd burned rubber on his way out of town, catching the best view of Coldwater he'd ever had—the one in his rearview mirror.

And now he was going back.

He followed the gentle curve of the two-lane blacktop, passing tin barns and mobile homes alternating with fields of cotton and corn and an occasional paint-starved farmhouse with a pickup truck out front. This corner of nowhere was home to people who didn't know there was a world beyond it. But he knew. He knew how a kid from nothing could leave a place like this and make something of himself. At the same time he burned with anger at how everything that same kid had fought so hard to gain could be ripped out from under him in the blink of an eye.

Cole still remembered how it felt to stand on that cold Dallas street in the middle of the night, soot clinging to his skin and heat from the massive blaze fanning his face, watching his half-finished real-estate renovation project—the one that could have made him a millionaire—light up the Dallas skyline like the fires of hell.

And watching his dreams go up in smoke with it.

He came around a bend and headed into the main part of town. He passed Blackwell's Pharmacy, A New You Dress Shop and Cut & Curl, where a handmade sign advertised twenty percent off acrylic nails on Tuesdays. When he reached Taffy's Restaurant, he pulled into a parking space next to a slick new pickup. It belonged to Ben Murphy, though he wouldn't have known that if not for the ancient hound dog hanging his head over the tailgate.

At least the old man had shown up.

Cole stepped out of his car, went to the back of Murphy's truck and scratched the old dog behind the ears.

"Hey, Duke. I figured you'd be long gone by now."

The dog licked his hand, and Cole smiled ruefully. Duke was far happier to see him than Murphy was going to be.

He gave the dog one last pat on the head, then turned toward the sidewalk. In the beauty-shop window next door, he saw a skinny brunette with a headful of rollers staring at him. She tapped a big-haired blonde on the shoulder and mouthed, *Cole McCallum.* The woman spun around, and when she caught sight of him her eyebrows flew halfway up to her hairline.

By the time he reached the door to the restaurant, the beauty-shop window was filled with half a dozen women in various states of beautification, from sopping wet hair to kinky hair to hair sprouting crinkles of silver stuff that looked like aluminum foil.

He couldn't resist. He turned toward the window and gave the ladies a great big smile.

A dozen eyes widened in unison. In the next second the women turned to each other, their mouths moving at the speed of light, probably repeating legends about him for the gospel truth whether they were actually true or not. Around here, any stranger made people stop and stare. But Cole McCallum, who was once rumored to have made it with the entire cheerleading squad in one night, warranted an all-points bulletin. And no doubt the things they'd read about him lately in the *Dallas Morning News* had only fueled the gossip.

He went into the restaurant and spotted Ben Murphy sitting in a booth by the far window. The chattering din of the restaurant fell silent as patrons peered over their newspapers or stopped mid-bite to watch him walk across the room. The only sound he heard was a hushed, rapid-fire argument behind the counter, where a trio of waitresses gave him sidelong glances as they tried to determine which took precedence when it came to waiting on a particular table—seniority or station assignments.

Cole slid into the booth across from Murphy and was greeted with a deadpan stare. The old man's jaw was set in stone, his blue eyes unreadable. All seventy-two of his years were etched into his face, solidified by the harsh Texas sun. He held a toothpick in the corner of his mouth, and Cole couldn't remember a time he'd seen him without one. Murphy was the closest thing to a grandfather he had by virtue of the fact that he'd married Cole's grandmother. That was where their relationship began—and ended.

A waitress appeared at the table, and it took Cole a moment to realize it was Mary Lou Culbertson, stuffed into a baby-blue waitress uniform that had probably been a really good fit ten years and twenty pounds ago. She cocked one hand against her hip and slid her other hand along the top of the booth behind him.

"Hey, Cole. Long time no see."

"Mary Lou."

"I read about you in the papers. You had a pretty tough time of it, didn't you?"

"It's over."

"Whatcha doin' back in town?"

"Taking care of a little business." He flashed her a smile. "How about a cup of coffee?"

"Sure." She purred the word, as if he'd just asked her to get naked in the back seat of his car. As she sashayed toward the coffeepot, Murphy raised an eyebrow.

"Still charming the ladies, I see."

Cole didn't reply. Instead he reached into his coat pocket and pulled out several legal-size sheets of paper. He opened them up and tossed them on the table.

Murphy eyed the papers. "I wondered if you'd be back. Cutting it a little close, aren't you?"

"According to Edna's will, as long as I'm married within six months of her death, then stay on the ranch with my wife for six months, the deed goes to me. The way I figure it, I have until Sunday to move in."

"You thumbed your nose at this six months ago. Said hell would freeze over before you got married and came back to live at the ranch."

Yeah, and six months ago he'd had money in the bank with big payoffs on the horizon. Now he had exactly nothing. He shrugged offhandedly. "People change."

"Some do. Some don't." Murphy chewed his toothpick. "And some become hotshot real estate investors who solve their problems with a book of matches."

Murphy's words slammed into Cole, making anger surge inside him. He struggled to keep his voice in check. "Guess you didn't read the paper two days ago. My partner was convicted. I wasn't."

Murphy shrugged. "So you had a better lawyer."

A hundred nasty retorts welled up inside Cole's mind, and it was all he could do to contain them. Nothing ever changed in this town. Nothing.

When he left Coldwater at age eighteen, he'd started renovating tiny, dilapidated houses, making a little money here and there and then rolling it over into bigger and bigger investments. Over the years, he amassed a large portfolio of rental property and a huge stash of cash.

Then, in a move that raised more than a few eyebrows, he and a partner bought Seven-Seventeen Broadway Avenue, a huge turn-of-the-century apartment building on the outskirts of downtown Dallas. The condition of the building left a lot to be desired, and the area was practically an abandoned ghetto, but the building had a period charm unlike any Cole had ever seen. Because of nearby renovation projects along with the growing desire of young urban pioneers for downtown addresses, he decided to take the risk and create luxury condominiums, hoping the yuppies would bite and other investors would follow suit.

Then came the fire.

Cole thought it was the worst thing that could possibly happen, until the blaze was ruled arson and he and his partner became prime suspects. Investigators speculated that they'd gotten concerned that their huge investment in such a questionable area wasn't going to pay off after all, so they'd torched it for the insurance money.

Cole had spent his last dime on the best attorneys he could buy, trying to convince a jury that he'd had nothing to do with the crime, all the while assuming his partner hadn't, either. Then it turned out the guy had a mountain of gambling debts Cole hadn't even known about, which had driven him to set the fire to try to collect the insurance money.

The fury Cole felt the moment he realized his partner's betrayal was superseded only by the gut-wrenching defeat he felt when he looked at that fire-ravaged lot. Because the fire had been deliberately set, the insurance company hadn't paid a dime, and Cole was left with nothing but a huge stack of attorney bills and a reputation that was in the toilet. Never mind that he'd been exonerated. The press had been quick to proclaim his alleged guilt on page one, then bury his innocence on page sixteen, and all the doors he'd worked so hard to open in the last ten years had suddenly slammed in his face.

Then he remembered his grandmother's will. He had one last shot to pull himself out financially and get back on top again, and he intended to take that shot—even if he had to spend another six months in Coldwater to do it.

"So where's the little woman?" Murphy asked. "Don't recall hearing anything about you getting married."

"She'll be here Sunday."

Cole held his breath, afraid Murphy was going to ask him more questions about his wife. Instead, he moved his toothpick to the other side of his mouth and gave Cole a warning stare.

"Part of the deal is that you work on the ranch."

"I've done it before."

"And hated every minute of it."

Cole couldn't argue with that. Still, he'd worked hard on the ranch the year he lived there, and Murphy knew it. Cole would have shot himself before giving the old man the satisfaction of telling Edna he wasn't pulling his weight.

Mary Lou put a cup of coffee down in front of Cole with a provocative smile. As she walked away, Cole shoved the cup aside.

"Edna's will allows me a monthly salary and the use of the foreman's house for the six months."

"That's what it says."

"Just wanted to make sure we're on the same track."

"We are, unless you're forgetting who decides whether you've stuck to the terms of the will. If you so much as forget to show up for work one day, I can call the whole thing off. What makes you think I'll cut you any slack?"

Good question. Cole knew Murphy didn't much like him showing up at the eleventh hour, because it meant another six months before the fate of the ranch would be decided. If Cole didn't inherit, Murphy would. Fortunately, Cole knew the ranch meant nothing to Murphy without Edna. And since Murphy had been financially well-off long before he and Edna got married, the money the ranch would bring at sale meant very little to him, anyway. But carrying out the stipulations of Edna's will meant everything to Murphy, whether he agreed with them or not.

"Because you're a fair man," Cole said. "Edna always said so."

Murphy's mouth twisted with irritation, and Cole knew he'd hit him where it hurt.

"Edna let her heart rule her head," Murphy said. "She knew her son was worthless, but his son—she had hope for him. Said all her grandson needed was a good woman, an honest job and something to work for, and he'd turn into a man she could be proud of. Instead you've spent the last year scraping to stay out of jail just like your old man."

Cole forced his expression to remain impassive, but he hardly felt that way inside. He remembered that day eleven years ago when a Dallas judge finally tossed his father in jail. At seventeen, Cole would have preferred to have been on his own, but the court hadn't seen it that way. His grandmother had agreed to take him in, and after a few rocky months, Cole made a surprising discovery—that at least one person in the world actually thought he might amount to something.

He knew she'd taken him in out of family responsibility, and in the beginning things had been pretty shaky. He remembered the day he arrived, so full of attitude that, looking back, he was surprised she hadn't kicked him right out the door. Instead, she'd fed him a hot meal, given him a clean bed to sleep in, then told him that no matter what his father had done, he wasn't his father and there was no need to follow in those footsteps.

In the coming months, no matter how many times he mouthed off, no matter how many times he screwed up, even though he could tell she was disappointed, still every day was a new day. Finally the days got better. She'd given him love and affection for the first time in his life, and when she died she left him everything—with a few strings attached. As her only living blood relative, the fact that she'd willed it all to him hadn't been a complete surprise. The terms of the will had.

"Now as for me," Murphy said, "I think Edna was dreaming. I think you're heading down the same road as your old man. Sure, you do things a little bigger and flashier, but the end result is the same. This is just a little detour along the way, like a trucker stopping to gas up. When you've got what you want, you'll be on the road again."

He stood up and tossed a five on the table, then lowered his voice. "One more thing. I made sure that nobody but you, me and the attorney who drew up the will knows anything about the provisions Edna outlined. If word gets out that she's trying to turn her no-good grandson into a hardworking family man, she's going to look like a fool, and I'll be damned if that's going to happen. If I think for one minute that you're telling people things they don't need to know, I'll pull the plug on this deal so fast it'll make your head spin. Now, do we understand each other?"

Cole nodded.

"See you Sunday. Looking forward to meeting the wife."

Cole watched him go, then sat back in the booth with a heavy sigh. Murphy was right about one thing. A year from now, when he sold the ranch and banked the money, his grandmother was going to look down from heaven and be sorely disappointed. But for all her good intentions, she hadn't understood that she could make him play the part of a hardworking husband, but she was never going to turn him into one.

This time last year, the mayor of Dallas himself had applauded Cole's efforts to revitalize a run-down area of town. *Dallas Monthly* had listed him as one of the twenty hottest bachelors in Dallas, which had given him so much instant celebrity that he couldn't even stop at 7-Eleven for a Big Gulp without a woman shoving her phone number into his pocket. And he'd been on the verge of making more money than he ever dreamed he would see in a lifetime. With the profit from the sale of the ranch, eventually he'd be able to get all of that back and then some. Why, then, would he want to waste his life away, saddled with a wife and kids, on a ranch in the middle of nowhere?

He stood up to leave, smiling broadly at the waitresses behind the counter. He added a quick wink, then listened to them chatter like a bunch of chipmunks as he walked out the door. He decided he would head over to the Lone Wolf Saloon on Highway 81. The place would fill up in an hour or so, providing him with the biggest assortment of women he was likely to find under one roof on short notice. He'd get a booth in the corner, order up a long neck, then sit back and do some serious shopping.

He had until tomorrow at midnight to find himself a wife.

VIRGINIA WHITE turned her 1993 Celica off the two-lane highway into a gas station, swung around the pumps and parked near the bathrooms on the west side. She grabbed the big shopping sack from the passenger seat beside her, hopped out of her car and got the bathroom key from the attendant.

She unlocked the bathroom door, hoping to find it clean, at least, only to see a stopped-up toilet, a wall of graffiti and half a dozen dead crickets on the floor. For a moment she wished she'd gone home to change clothes, but it was twenty-one miles from the outlet mall back to Coldwater. If she'd done that she would have lost her nerve altogether and ended up staying home.

She locked the door and nudged the crickets behind the toilet with the toe of her canvas shoe. She shimmied out of the dumpy flowered dress her mother had bought her at a garage sale last summer and stuffed it into the trash can. She removed her white cotton bra and disposed of it, too, then pulled out of the sack the one part of her purchase that she'd barely had the nerve to buy—a black lace push-up bra with a front clasp, dainty satin straps and enough padding to stuff a mattress.

Cheap women wear bras like that, her mother had always said. *Cheap little hussies who are looking for trouble.*

Virginia put it on, then turned to the mirror and froze.

Cleavage. For the first time in her life, she actually had cleavage.

She stared at the cheap little hussy in the mirror and held her breath, her heart beating double time, waiting, waiting...

Finally she slumped with relief. Okay. God hadn't struck her dead. That was a good sign. Maybe her mother didn't have half the pull with the Almighty that she'd always led Virginia to believe, even though she'd been up there with Him now for over three months, consulting with Him in person.

Virginia pulled a pair of jeans from the sack and wiggled into them, thinking maybe they looked pretty good for her first pair. At $12.99 they hadn't eaten her whole paycheck, and they had a little strip of elastic in the back so, even though they were sort of tight, she'd still be able to breathe.

Next she pulled out a brown short-sleeved cotton shirt with little horseshoes on it. Very Western. She put it on, leaving the top two buttons undone. On second thought, she unbuttoned a third one, then spread the edges of the shirt apart to reveal a hint of her newly enhanced bustline. She froze again, holding her breath, waiting for the inevitable. But it never came.

Maybe God was fresh out of thunderbolts.

She pulled a pair of plain brown cowboy boots from the sack and tugged them on, knowing they couldn't possibly be leather for $17.99, but figuring they looked the part, anyway. Turning to the mirror, she ran a brush through her hair, wishing for the umpteenth time in her life that she'd been blessed with wavy blond tresses instead of the limp brown mop she'd gotten stuck with. Then she pulled a tube of lipstick from the sack. It wasn't the cherry red she'd planned on getting, but it wasn't baby pink, either. She spent a good five minutes nose-to-nose with her reflection in the mirror, dabbing at her lips, telling herself it was just like kindergarten and all she had to do was color inside the lines.

She smacked her lips together, then backed off from the mirror for an arm's-length exam. Okay. Not bad. Truth be told, though, she didn't much care what she looked like.

As long as she didn't look like Virginia White.

A few minutes later she was back on the blacktop, moving down the road. She rolled down the windows and jacked up the radio, singing along with Shania Twain. The crisp breeze lifted her hair off the back of her neck. The sun had just set, filling the countryside with the muted shades of twilight. It would be dark by the time she reached her destination.

Happy birthday, Virginia, she told herself. *It's time to go live it up.*

Tonight she was giving herself a long overdue gift. She was going someplace where there were hundreds of people she didn't know. People to whom her name meant nothing. People who wouldn't automatically dismiss her because she was the daughter of the town recluse, or because she didn't dress right, or because she was just a painfully shy nobody who'd never learned how to be anything else.

While she'd been working at the library after school to help support her and her mother, other girls were chatting on the phone, painting each other's nails and talking about boys. While she was paying bills and balancing the checkbook, other girls were making out in the back seats of cars. While she was living with her mother, taking care of her various ailments and catering to her whims, other women were getting married, making love and having children.

Sooner or later she would save enough money for college, and then she'd start a whole new life. But bank tellers didn't make much, particularly when they worked at the First State Bank of Coldwater, Texas, where raises came around about as often as Halley's Comet. So it could take a while, maybe even a couple of years, and she couldn't wait that long to start grabbing some of the fun and excitement the rest of the world took for granted.

She kept singing along with Shania, letting her foot get heavy on the gas pedal until she teetered on the edge of the forty-five-mile-per-hour speed limit. Then, just as she was starting to feel pretty cool, she topped a hill and her destination came into sight, and she felt self-conscious all over again.

The Lone Wolf Saloon was nothing more than a gigantic, flat-sided metal building with its name on the side in red-and-blue neon. But looks were deceiving. From what Virginia had heard, it was sitting smack-dab in the middle of the fast lane of life, offering a wild, rowdy evening of decadence to every fun-loving person within a thirty-mile radius.

The gravel parking lot was nearly full. Virginia found a space between a pair of spit-polished, fresh-off-the-lot pickup trucks. She turned off the engine and sat in silence for a moment, hearing her mother's voice reverberating inside her head.

Places like that ought to be outlawed. They're sinful, that's what they are. Sinful.

She took a few deep, calming breaths, telling herself that if going out and having a good time was a sin, hell would be so full by now that there wouldn't be any room for her, anyway.

She grabbed her purse, eased out of her car and locked it behind her. She toddled across the gravel parking lot as best she could in her new footwear and made it to the front door. She squared her shoulders, bracing herself against the unknown, but still she was unprepared for the sensory overload that assaulted her the moment she opened the door.

The music, played by a country-western band gyrating

with wild enthusiasm on a rainbow-lit stage, hit her ear-drums at approximately a hundred decibels above the super-sonic range. Every chord, every drumbeat, every twang of the lead singer's voice hummed through her body like an electri-cal circuit gone haywire. A beer. That's what she needed.

She headed toward the bar, passing table after table crowded with people and littered with beer bottles and ash-trays. The entire place seemed to be in motion, from the slow rhythm of interaction between men and women, to the sway of denim and leather on the dance floor, to the slither of wait-resses from one table to the next. Every molecule of air was drenched in cigarette smoke, giving the room a surreal, oth-erworldly feel. Virginia had a thought about secondhand smoke, then chastised herself. She'd spent twenty-four years breathing the right air, so one evening of sucking in a few car-cinogens was hardly going to matter.

She found an empty bar stool and climbed onto it. The bar-tender, a brawny beast with biceps the size of telephone poles, approached her. He wore a single gold earring that glinted under the neon lights surrounding the bar.

She cleared her throat. "A beer, please?"

"Any particular kind?"

Virginia froze. "In a bottle?"

The bartender gave her a sarcastic little smile and walked away, leaving her feeling dumb as a rock. To her relief, though, he returned a moment later and slapped a bottle on the bar in front of her. "Three bucks."

She gave the bartender three one-dollar bills, then picked up the beer. It felt ice-cold. She sniffed it tentatively, then put the bottle to her lips and took a sip. She swallowed, and her eyes started to water. It was like drinking a rancid, extra-fizzy soda, but she managed to get it down without it coming back up. Buoyed by that small victory, she took another sip, this time a bigger one, and felt it burn all the way down her throat.

Okay. That wasn't so bad. And because she was still among the living, she decided maybe God was taking the weekend off.

She took mini-sips of the beer and turned around on the bar stool to watch the crowd. Nobody seemed to notice her, which was pretty much par for the course. She was one of those people who didn't speak up, who blended into the woodwork, who got lost in a crowd of two. It had been that way all her life, and she didn't expect things would change overnight.

As long as they changed eventually.

The couples on the dance floor moved with intricate little steps and whirls, their feet always falling in just the right places. Then a dozen or so people lined up to do a little group dance, where everybody seemed to know just where to step to avoid kicking the person in front of them.

And everywhere, people were laughing.

Pretty soon Virginia started to loosen up, and by the time she'd drained the bottle, she felt warm and a little woozy. She ordered another one, thinking if one made her feel good, two would be even better.

Then the band played a soft, soulful number. Couples inched closer to each other, body-to-body, moving together as one. Virginia felt as if the world had suddenly paired up two by two and she was the odd woman out.

She rested her elbow on the bar, her cheek against her palm, watching all the lucky women who knew what it felt like to ease next to a man, tuck their heads against a broad shoulder and move to the music, letting the rest of the world slip away. A wave of longing swept through her that was so powerful she thought she'd faint from the feeling.

Not once in her life had a man so much as touched her.

She'd never been on a date, never been kissed, never chatted with a girlfriend about boys. She'd never had a man look into her eyes with desire or tell her she was beautiful. She wasn't, of course. They didn't come any plainer than Virginia White, so she had to face facts. She was going to need a little extra *something* that didn't involve a traffic-stopping body or a Miss America smile.

Maybe it was all in the way a woman moved. That was apparently what a platinum blonde on the dance floor right now thought as she undulated against her partner. Making love standing up. That's what it looked like. Not that Virginia knew the details of such a thing, but even a cloistered nun could see what that woman had in mind.

Virginia couldn't say she blamed her.

If she'd been dancing with a man as sexy as that woman's partner, it might make her hormones shift into overdrive, too. He was tall, well over six feet, moving to the music as if he'd been born to do it. Virginia inhaled the sight of him, her gaze traveling from his rock-solid shoulders, to his narrow waist, to his hips and thighs swaying rhythmically inside a pair of snug, well-worn jeans. Thick, dark hair brushed the back of his shirt collar, and she watched as the blonde eased her hands upward and threaded her fingers through it. Virginia wondered what that would feel like. She wondered what all of it would feel like—dancing, touching, even kissing. She blushed at the very thought of it, but that didn't stop her mind from wandering into previously uncharted territory. Then he turned, and she had a sudden, stunning view of an incredibly handsome face.

She blinked. It couldn't be.

Cole McCallum.

She felt a hot rush at the realization of just who it was she was looking at. It had been a lot of years since she'd seen him, but he wasn't the kind of guy you easily forgot. She'd been a freshman when he was a senior, but still she'd fantasized about him, even though good girls weren't supposed to have the hots for bad boys. Not that it would have mattered which way her hots were directed. A guy like Cole McCallum would never have been interested in a shy, dumpy little wallflower who would have gone into cardiac arrest if he'd so much as glanced in her direction.

Maybe it was a good thing he'd never looked her way. If there was one thing she'd learned by keeping her mouth shut and her ears open, it was that Cole's good looks and ladykilling smile were nothing more than bait for any unsuspecting girl who happened to wander into his web.

The band wrapped up the song and Cole left the dance floor, the blonde clinging to him like moss on a tree. Age had only improved him, turning a cocky, hell-raising, sexylooking teenager into a smooth, confident, sexy-looking man. She couldn't say for sure if the hell-raising part still applied, but she doubted that inclination had left him entirely.

Virginia caught the bartender's eye and ordered another beer, and before long the room began to spin in a most pleasant manner. She closed her eyes and listened hard, but the alcohol had chased away her mother's voice. She drained the beer and set the empty bottle on the bar with a definitive clunk. Warmth coursed through her all the way to her toes, and she sighed with contentment.

For the first time in her life she felt free.

Nobody was standing over her shoulder passing judgment. Nobody was telling her what to think. Nobody was soliciting thunderbolts from the heavens as a punishment for the slightest transgression. She was in charge of her own destiny and answered to no one.

She watched Cole dance with another woman, following his tall, gorgeous body like a moth follows light. Beer number three hit home, and she started to think that maybe there wasn't that much difference between her and those other women he seemed so interested in. It was possible, wasn't it, that she might even have some qualities they didn't?

A boldness she'd never felt before unfurled inside her like a tight rosebud opening to the sun. As the minutes ticked by, she started to feel less like a wallflower and more like a woman who could rule the world. She rose from her bar stool, wobbling a little, but never losing sight of the opportunity that was staring her right in the face.

Maybe a bad boy like Cole McCallum was exactly what this good girl needed.

2

COLE TOOK a sip from his long neck, settled back in his chair and surveyed the situation. It didn't look good.

The Lone Wolf was filled to capacity, teeming with Friday nightlife. He'd been here several times before, years ago. Even though he'd been underage through most of that time, he'd never had any trouble getting in the door. Even at seventeen he'd looked twenty-one, standing six-foot-two with an attitude even taller, tempered by a killer smile he'd learned early to use to his advantage. And he'd be willing to put it to good use right now, if only he could find that one special woman who wouldn't mind being married for six months and then disappearing.

In the glove compartment of his car was the necessary prenuptial agreement that would allow him to sidestep Texas community property laws, along with the phone numbers of a couple of the airlines so he could snag some last-minute tickets to Vegas tomorrow night. But the woman...now that was going to be a bigger problem than he anticipated.

Not that he didn't already have a few candidates. Within ten minutes of his arrival, three ladies had made themselves at home at his table. The first had been Tonya Jenkins, a bleach blonde who'd graduated from Coldwater High the same year he had and now lived in Tyler. She wore a denim miniskirt and fringed leather vest that closed over her ample breasts with a single tie—without the benefit of a shirt beneath it. Everything about her was excessive, from the height of her oversprayed hair to the makeup she'd applied with a steamroller, to the way she kept running her bloodred fingernails up and down his arm. He remembered now it was because of Tonya that he'd developed such an aversion to pushy women.

She grabbed his hand. "C'mon, Cole. Let's dance."

She had that look of hot anticipation on her face that told him if he so much as raised an eyebrow, she'd have her skirt up and her panties down in a heartbeat.

He maintained an easygoing smile. "Think I'll sit this one out."

"But you danced with Shelly and Tiffany." She pressed that cherry-red bottom lip of hers into a full pout, and he could tell his mission tonight was going to be a much bigger challenge than he'd anticipated.

He'd tried to look up some of the women he knew in Dallas to see if any of them might be interested in a temporary marriage, but without exception they'd moved on to other eligible bachelors months ago when they discovered he had an arson accusation hanging over his head. So he jumped into his car and headed here, figuring a local girl might make a better candidate anyway. Someone from around here would be more likely to submit to life on a ranch for six months, while the women he knew in Dallas would last about a week before they burst into tears and rushed back to the city for a trip to Neiman Marcus and lunch at the Palm.

The downside of marrying a girl from the Coldwater area was that it pretty much insured that Murphy would find out the marriage wasn't the real thing. But according to the provisions of the will, as long as Cole got married by midnight tomorrow night and he and his bride spent six months on the ranch as man and wife, Murphy couldn't pull the plug on the deal just because they weren't committed to a lifetime relationship. At the end of that time period, Cole would sell the ranch, give his new ex-wife twenty-five thousand dollars for her trouble, then take the rest of the proceeds and get on with the life he was meant to live.

He surveyed the women at his table. Shelly was a definite possibility. She was decent looking, with platinum blond hair and a pair of breasts that were beyond belief. A few quick questions had netted him the answers he needed to move forward. No, she wasn't married; no, she wasn't thinking of leaving town anytime soon; and yes, she was a spontaneous person. Unfortunately she seemed about as bright as a two-watt bulb.

Tiffany, on the other hand, had at least a few gears turning upstairs. She had dark, silky hair, a pair of mile-long legs and seemed to be open to new adventures, but at the same time she was quick to say she'd just come off a nasty divorce. Marriage to a man with an ulterior motive might not sit too well with her.

The more he looked at them, though, the more he sensed a harshness about them that turned him off—a shadowed, wary look in their eyes that said they'd been around the block a time or two and could easily shift into ball buster mode if need be. Could he spend six months in the same house with a woman like that?

And then there was Tonya.

He checked his watch. Time was running short, and his options were few. He had to make a decision pretty quickly, because if one turned him down, he'd need time to talk another one into it. But which one first? Would they think it was strange if he asked them to draw straws?

"Excuse me?"

He looked up from his beer to see a woman standing in front of his table. Just barely a woman. He couldn't say for sure she was even of legal age to be there. She wore a shirt with little horseshoes all over it, and her jeans were a deep indigo blue with a loose, crinkly fit. If she added a straw hat and a bandanna, she'd look just like Dale Evans.

Her brown eyes shifted back and forth as she systematically disintegrated a balled-up cocktail napkin, and he got the feeling that if he so much as said boo she'd go running for the hills. He pictured her going out with guys who wore sweater-vests and had her home by ten o'clock—the kind of date she could bring home to Mom for Sunday dinner. But here she was at a raunchy country-western bar on a Friday night looking as out of place as a sparrow in a flock of peacocks.

Then she fixed her gaze on his, and he felt a twinge of apprehension. She took a deep, shaky breath, looking as if she were about to faint.

"Would you like to dance?" she asked.

Oh, boy. He did *not* need this.

Before he could say anything, though, Tonya snickered a little, then leaned forward, her forearms on the table. "A little out of your league, aren't you, honey?"

For a minute Cole thought the woman might go running for the hills after all. Instead she stood her ground, but her slightly panicked expression said it was a hard-won battle.

Tonya smelled blood. "Don't you have a church social to go to? Or how about a bingo game? I hear it's twenty-dollar jackpot night down at the VFW Hall."

To her credit, the woman didn't respond. She weaved a little, and Cole wondered if maybe she hadn't had one beer too many. Then she lifted her chin, and in a shaky voice she asked him again if he'd like to dance.

The other women exchanged glances, laughing behind their hands. God, he hated this. There was nothing worse than an arrogant shrew like Tonya picking on somebody who didn't have the guts to give it right back to her. The woman's eyes were getting a little shiny. If he didn't do something, in just a few seconds Tonya was *really* going to have something to laugh about.

He sighed inwardly and gave the woman a big smile. "Sure, sweetheart. I'd love to dance."

In unison, three female jaws hit the ground. He rose from the booth and took the woman's hand, then parted the crowd and led her to the dance floor.

"Look out, Cole," Tonya called. "She's obviously a loose woman. Liable to ruin your reputation."

The other women laughed, but Cole ignored them. He heard more snide remarks, which he likewise ignored. One quick dance, and then he could return to the business at hand.

The band was playing a mournful somebody-done-me-wrong song just perfect for slow dancing. When they reached the dance floor he pulled her around to face him. She froze, her eyes wide.

"You want to dance, don't you?" he asked.

She nodded.

"Then what's the matter?"

She mumbled something he couldn't make out.

He leaned closer to her. "What?"

"I—I said I don't know how to dance."

Great. Now he was a dance instructor.

He thought about excusing himself and heading to the bar for another beer, but then the catcalls would only get louder and she'd probably end up crying, and he figured nobody ought to have to go through that. She stared at him, her liquid brown eyes making her look like a baby doe who'd wandered into a cougar's den.

"There's nothing to it," he told her, stepping closer. "Just put your arms around my neck."

When she didn't move, he took her hands and draped them over his shoulders. She circled them around his collar, her touch featherlight. He slipped his arms around her waist, and she inched closer to him. He started to move a little, letting her get the feel of it, but she was as stiff as a fence post. It was like dancing with a two-by-four.

"Loosen up, sweetheart." He flattened his palm against the small of her back and moved it in slow circles. He worked his hand up and down her back, rubbing the tension away, at the same time easing her closer.

"Good. That's good. Now all you have to do is follow me. Just listen to the music and move along with it."

Slowly she started to get the hang of it. As inept as she was, he had to admit it was a welcome relief from Shelly and Tiffany. To them, dancing was nothing more than vertical foreplay. They moved their silicone-amplified figures all over him as if they expected him to drop to the floor and have sex with them on the spot.

Not this one. She was soft and round and warm as toast, and he had the feeling that if he squeezed her too hard she just might break. She had hair the color of a paper sack, but it was the color God gave her and full of shine, and when he brushed his fingers over it, it felt as soft as dandelion fuzz.

"Am I doing it right?" she asked, staring at his chest.

"You're doing just fine."

"I don't want to step on your feet."

There wasn't much of her, so he probably wouldn't know it even if she did. "You won't step on my feet. In fact, I can't even tell this is your first time dancing."

To his surprise, she inched closer and rested her cheek against his shoulder. Her head fit perfectly into the crook of his neck. As they moved to the music, he dipped his head a little and caught the scent of peach shampoo instead of being assaulted by a wave of cheap perfume. She sighed gently, and the last of her tension seemed to drain right out of her, leaving her warm and pliant in his arms. He ran his hands along her spine, down to the stretchy waistband of those oddball jeans of hers, then up to her neck, and she shifted beneath his hands and melted into him. It had been a long time since he'd danced with a woman who wasn't auditioning for a roll in the hay, and it felt...nice.

Nice enough to be married to her for six months?

The thought came into his head in a flash, and just as quickly he sent it packing. She'd be horrified at the very thought of a temporary marriage. Women like this one met their soul mates in the church choir, dated for five years, then planned a wedding complete with doves, rice bags and a silver punch bowl. They did not sign a prenup, get married at the Elvis Memorial Wedding Chapel in Vegas, then spend their six-month anniversary getting a divorce.

After a couple of minutes the song wound down. She looked at him, blinking as if she'd just awakened from a very pleasant dream. He had the fleeting thought that he might be wearing the same expression.

He started to move away from her, thinking maybe he ought to suggest that this wasn't the place for a woman like her, when suddenly she took a double handful of his shirt and pulled him against her. She closed her eyes. "Kiss me."

"Excuse me?"

"Kiss me." A note of desperation crept into her voice. "Please?"

Cole stared at her, dumbfounded. But after the initial shock wore off, he realized that the thought of fulfilling that request wasn't entirely without appeal, but for the life of him he couldn't figure out why. His taste in women ran toward the experienced type, women who gave a lot but didn't take too much and knew how to say goodbye before breakfast.

So why wasn't he pushing her away?

A pink flush rose on her cheeks, and her chest heaved gently as she looked at him with pleading eyes. She wanted this badly. He was no stranger to women's desires, but something told him there was more involved here than a little elemental lust.

"Look, sweetheart, maybe you'd better—"

"Would you do it for a hundred dollars?"

"*What?*"

"I—I hear you're worth it."

He almost laughed, but she sounded so serious that he caught it before it came out. "So you know who I am?"

She nodded.

Cole sighed. More proof that his legend lived on.

He took her by the shoulders and looked at her as platonically as he knew how. "Now, look. I'm not arguing the value of my services, and I don't remember a time in my life when I turned down easy money—"

"So you'll do it?"

"No!"

She sighed, then circled her gaze around the room. "That's okay, I guess. There's bound to be somebody else here—"

Cole clamped his hand onto her forearm and hauled her off the dance floor, pulling her toward the opposite side of the room. When he reached a secluded spot next to the bar, he backed her up against the wall beneath a neon beer advertisement.

"Now, listen up! It's not a good idea to go flashing a bunch of cash in a bar full of drunk cowboys, offering to pay them to do something that's liable to turn into something else!"

"Something else?"

Good God. How had this woman survived life so far? He stared at her pointedly.

She looked away. "Oh. That."

"Yes, *that*, maybe whether you want it or not. You don't want to tangle with some of these guys, especially the closer it gets to closing time."

Closing time. It was a little after eight now. He'd better get a move on if he expected to make a decision on a fiancée, or it was going to be a *really* short engagement.

"Maybe it would be best if you headed on home," he said. "The later it gets around here, the rowdier it gets. It's not a good place for a nice girl—"

"Don't say that!"

Cole stepped back, startled. Those soft brown eyes were suddenly shooting fire.

"I'm *not* a nice girl! I mean, I am, but I don't want to be!" She glanced at the bartender, a six-foot-three, two-hundred-pound slab of beef who was simultaneously drawing a beer and eyeing a brunette whose tank top was working overtime trying to contain her generous upper body. "That bartender is a possibility, I guess. Maybe I'll ask him—"

"No!"

Cole pulled her around, wondering if her problem was confined to naïveté or whether there was an unhealthy dose of insanity thrown in. "I don't get it. Why in the world would you pay a man to kiss you?"

She shrugged a little and looked at her feet, which she didn't seem to be too steady on at the moment. "Because I want to know what it feels like."

For a minute Cole wasn't sure he'd heard her right. Then all at once the truth hit him like a brick to the side of the head. "You've never been kissed before?"

She continued her examination of those weird-looking boots of hers, her cheeks the color of ripe strawberries, and he had his answer.

Good Lord. How had this happened? How did any woman get through puberty and adolescence and into adulthood without so much as a kiss? Sure, she was plain, but he'd seen far less attractive women who'd managed to hook a man. How had things gone so wrong when it was so easy to make them right?

Then he pictured her sidling up next to that bruiser of a bartender and making him the same offer. Either the man would laugh his head off and humiliate her or take advantage of the situation in ways Cole didn't even want to think about.

"I heard something once about six cheerleaders," the woman said, her blush deepening. "I figured one little kiss wouldn't be a big deal."

Damn, was that story carved in granite somewhere? If so, it was time he found a stick of dynamite and did away with it permanently.

"Two things," Cole told her. "First of all, don't believe everything you hear. And secondly, a kiss *is* a big deal. Especially if you've never done it before."

Those liquid brown eyes came up to meet his. They weren't exactly beautiful—nothing about her was—but something about the way she stared at him made his throat feel tight and muddled up his thinking. Her lips parted slightly, and she touched the tip of her tongue to her lower lip, leaving it damp and glistening. There was nothing deliberately seductive about it, and maybe that's why it was so...seductive.

Pay attention, Tonya. You're about to get an eyeful.

"Kissing is like dancing," he told her softly, moving his hands up to cradle her face. "You just do what comes naturally."

She stared at him with that look of terror again, swallowing as if there were a golf ball lodged in her throat. He thought of getting it over with quickly to put her out of her misery, but then again, if she was after a hundred-dollar kiss, he figured that's what he ought to give her.

He brushed his lips against hers. Her cheeks were tense, her jaw fixed, her mouth a firm, unyielding line.

"Relax," he said. "This is supposed to be fun."

He met her lips again, but this time he persisted, fixing his mouth firmly over hers until she had no choice but to give in.

He stroked his thumbs along her cheekbones, feeling skin as soft as powder.

Then he wrapped his arm around the back of her neck and cradled her head in the crook of his elbow. He tilted her backward slightly, and at the same time he brought his other hand down to circle her rib cage just beneath her breast.

She gasped a little at his touch, parting her lips at the same time, and he took the opportunity to delve deeper. He teased the tip of his tongue against her lips in gentle exploration, then slipped it into her mouth and twined it softly with hers. He could feel her surprise, as if she'd never imagined kissing could involve something like *that.* But a moment later she slid one hand around his neck and the other over his shoulder, pulling him closer, asking for more, as if she'd just tasted an unknown delicacy and couldn't get enough of it. Her eager response sent a jolt of awareness through him, and all at once he realized that if she'd never been kissed, then that meant she also hadn't—

No. He'd never made love to a virgin, and he wasn't about to start now. Too damn much responsibility there. But kissing one? Now that was another thing entirely. A thing he hadn't realized could be quite so...enjoyable.

He moved his hand to the small of her back and pulled her tightly against him, her breasts crushed to his chest, heat coursing from her body to his. He thought he heard a catcall or two in the background, but he ignored the crowd and the raucous music and the flashing lights around them, making sure that from now on she'd know exactly what a hundred-dollar kiss felt like.

Then her knees buckled a little, and out of fear that she might actually pass out, he finally pulled away, his arm still wrapped around her back holding her snugly against him. Slowly she opened her eyes, wearing a glassy-eyed, thoroughly *kissed* expression that sent a shock wave right to his groin.

"I lied," she said. "I don't have a hundred dollars."

"Then I guess I'll have to take the kiss back."

He pressed his lips to hers again in an impulsive reprise of the already thorough kiss he'd just given her. A quick start of surprise on her part immediately gave way to surrender. By now she had one kiss under her belt, moving her ahead in the amateur ranks, and this time she met him with far less fear and far more enthusiasm.

Finally he pulled away. She closed her eyes and let out a rapturous little sigh, her arms still draped around his neck. She was an amateur, yes, but he hadn't expected her to have so much potential. Warm, willing and totally untouched—what would it be like to find a woman like that lying naked in his bed?

If he married her, he could find out.

No. That was crazy. Just kissing her had probably put him in danger of her daddy coming after him with a shotgun, and the last thing he needed right now was a major complication like that.

"Look, sweetheart. I think it's time for you to—"

All at once her eyes sprang open, her expression becoming tense, her eyes growing wider by the moment.

"What's the matter?" Cole asked.

She backed away from him, one hand on her stomach, the other clutching his arm. Her eyes glazed over, and her face turned as pale as an eggshell. He'd seen that look before.

"How many drinks did you have?"

"Uh...two. No. Three."

"Is that three more than you've ever had before?"

"Uh-huh." She wobbled a little, hunched over, and in her next breath everything that had gone down tonight came right back up.

VIRGINIA DECIDED there was nothing quite so inelegant as sitting on the bathroom floor of a sleazy country-western bar, hugging a toilet and staring at a wall full of graffiti describing sex acts she didn't even think were anatomically possible. She'd barely gotten the little paper sanitary thing down on the toilet seat before she'd thrown up all over again.

She folded her arms on the edge of the toilet and rested her forehead against them, wishing the bumblebees in her stomach would head back to the hive. God had evidently gotten more creative than in the Old Testament days. What did He need with a thunderbolt? All He had to do was get her to toss down three beers and throw up at Cole McCallum's feet. She may not be dead, but she certainly wished she was.

She couldn't believe she'd had the nerve to ask Cole to dance, much less what came after. Of course, she had to admit that right now the majority of her courage lay in an unmentionable heap on the barroom floor. That explained her actions. But why had Cole taken her up on it?

The only reason was that he was exactly what she'd always heard—a wild, sexually insatiable animal who didn't care where he got his kicks. Logically, that made sense. Somehow, though, the kisses hadn't felt that way at all. They had felt warm and wonderful and exciting, and she'd wanted them to go on forever.

But maybe that was part of the game he played. He was gorgeous and charming and highly talented in the kissing department, and that's what made him so dangerous. He'd grown into a man with ten years more experience in compromising women, and in that time he'd obviously sharpened his tools to a fine edge.

Men are after only one thing, she heard her mother saying in that chastising voice that had reappeared in her head about the time she headed for the bathroom. *And once they get it, they'll be gone.*

She had to admit that her mother was somewhat of an expert on that subject. Virginia had never known her father. Her mother had—for one night. And her whole life Virginia had been a daily reminder to her mother of the mistake she'd made in trusting a man, and she never missed the opportunity to warn her daughter not to follow in her footsteps.

Virginia flicked a cigarette butt off her thigh and got up, thinking maybe it was finally safe to move farther than arm's length away from the toilet. She left the stall, wobbled to the mirror and stifled a scream. Her hair hung in limp strings, her lipstick had melted away, and every fleck of color had fled from her face. She looked like a bag lady with anemia.

Then she had a terrible thought. What if Cole was still out there? The last thing she wanted to do was humiliate herself all over again by tripping over her own feet or teetering back and forth like an acrobat on a high wire.

The only way she could hold on to her last few shreds of self-respect was to walk out to that bar, preferably in a straight line, find her purse if it hadn't been stolen, then go home and forget this night had ever been. And if she saw Cole, she'd simply say good-night calmly and offhandedly as if none of this—from his earth-shattering kisses to her involuntary recycling of three bottles of beer—had been any big deal at all.

"YOU SHOULDN'T have let your girlfriend drink that much."

Cole glared at the bartender. "She's not my girlfriend."

"Whatever. I just want her out of here. Puking customers are bad for business. Where does she live?"

"I never met her before tonight. I have no idea where she lives."

The bartender slapped a purse onto the bar in front of Cole. "Find out."

Cole spit out a disgusted breath and unzipped Virginia's purse. He hauled out a notepad, a checkbook, a pink plastic thing containing feminine hygiene products and one of those little blue-and-white packets of tissues. Finally he located her wallet and pulled out her driver's license.

Virginia White. Seven-fourteen Oakdale. Coldwater, Texas.

Damn. Coldwater was a good twenty miles from here. The chances of her making it home without ending up in a ditch or wrapped around a tree were approximately zero.

"What are you doing with my purse?"

Cole looked up to see Virginia staggering toward him. She was even paler than before, her eyes heavy-lidded, and she seemed to be having a hard time focusing.

"You live in Coldwater?" he asked her.

"Yeah."

"That's twenty miles from here. You can't drive home."

"Of course I can drive home."

She grabbed for her purse, but Cole pulled it out of her reach. He fished out her car keys and stuffed them into his pocket.

"What are you doing?"

"Any woman who can't hold three beers ought to have her license revoked." He reached into his other pocket, extracted some change and slapped it into her palm. "There's a phone by the front door. Go call someone to come get you."

She stared at him blankly.

"A friend? Relative?"

She shrugged.

"You mean there's no one you can call?"

"It's no concern of yours. Now, may I have my keys?"

She was right. It was no concern of his. She wasn't his problem. So why didn't he just order another beer, forget he'd ever met her and move on to more important matters?

She held out her hand, her mouth a firm line of determination, but he could tell from her bloodshot eyes and the way she swayed like a willow in a light breeze that she'd be lucky to make it to the front door. A tiny shred of decency he would have sworn he didn't have nagged at him like an itch in the middle of his back he couldn't quite reach.

Cole rubbed his eyes with the heels of his hands, then let out a disgusted breath. He crammed her belongings into her purse and thrust it at her. "Come on. We're leaving."

"What?"

"I'm taking you home."

"That won't be necessary. I said I'm quite able to drive."

"Yeah. Right into a telephone pole."

"No. I'm an excellent driver." Her testiness almost offset the drunken slur in her voice. "I made a hundred percent on my driver's test when I turned sixteen."

"You think a cop's gonna care about that when he stops you?"

"I have a perfect driving record. I've never had an accident. I've never even had a parking ticket."

Cole wanted to beat his head against the bar. "You're full of alcohol!"

"Not completely."

She was right about that. "You're still drunk, though. Believe me."

"Yes. Well. Comparatively speaking, that would simply make me a mediocre driver. The road is full of mediocre drivers. Do they take every one of them to jail?"

He'd already determined she was both naive and insane. Now he could add illogical to the list.

She held out her hand. "My keys?"

"Fine." Cole pulled her keys from his pocket and slapped them into her hand.

"Thank you very much," she said, with a queenly nose-in-the-air thing that really irritated him. She swung her purse over her shoulder in a wild arc, the momentum practically knocking her over. She righted herself, took a deep breath and started for the door.

"Have a nice drive," Cole called. "Of course, the minute you're out the door I'm calling the cops and giving them your license number. And after you walk that little white line, you'll spend the night in the drunk tank."

She turned around, her eyes wide. "Drunk tank?"

"Yeah. Right after they strip-search you."

Her mouth dropped open. "*Strip*-search?"

"Don't worry. If they get too carried away, you can always sue. You have a good lawyer, don't you?"

She squeezed her eyes closed and slumped with resignation. "What about my car? If you take me home, it'll still be here in the morning."

"That's your problem." Cole put a firm hand against her

shoulder and turned her toward the door. "I'll get you home in one piece. Past that, you're on your own."

Shelly's, Tiffany's and Tonya's eyes flew open with disbelief as he passed by their table, his arm wrapped around Virginia's shoulders, dragging her along. He took her to his car, unlocked the passenger door, then shook a finger at her. "Don't you *dare* throw up in my car."

"I won't."

Her words said she wouldn't, but her sickly expression said it was a distinct possibility. That would be the last straw, of course. If she messed up his car, he wouldn't think twice about tossing her out on the side of the road and letting the buzzards have at her.

He opened the door. She collapsed on the seat, but that's as far as she got. He picked her legs up, stuffed them into the car and slammed the door.

He slid behind the wheel and jammed the key into the ignition. He was saving her from driving drunk. That was a good deed. Good deeds were supposed to make a person feel wonderful.

Yeah. Right.

He checked his watch. He had only a few hours left. He didn't need someone throwing a wrench in the works, and he had a feeling Virginia White had a whole toolbox in her hip pocket. He intended to dump her at home, turn around and head back to the bar.

Twenty minutes later he pulled up to 714 Oakdale, a tiny white clapboard house on a tree-shaded street. It was one of those houses that had been born ugly, with a flat elevation, an aluminum storm door and casement windows. Still, it was well-kept, with a neat St. Augustine lawn, a bed of pink petunias and a wreath beside the front door. At least somebody was trying.

Virginia had fallen asleep about two minutes after getting

into his car, and she still slept, breathing gently, her hands clutching her purse, her lips parted. A stray strand of hair lay across her cheek. She looked peaceful. Innocent. Helpless. The kind of woman he vowed he'd never go near again.

No lights shone in any of the windows. She lived alone, he guessed, or she'd have called someone to come pick her up. He slipped her keys out of her hand and unlocked the front door. He came around the car and pulled her out. He tried walking her toward the porch without much success, then gave up and picked her up. He climbed the porch steps with her in his arms, nudged the storm door open with his foot and flipped on the living-room light with his shoulder. He carried her into the first bedroom he came to, those goofy boots of hers banging against the door frame. He dumped her on the bed, then yanked her boots off.

A quilt lay folded at the end of the bed, and he pulled it over her. She turned on her side, squirmed around for a minute, then hugged the pillow and played dead. And dead was just how she was going to feel in the morning.

Cole went into the living room. The house was stuck in a time warp. Green shag carpet, heavy gold drapes, brown plaid furniture. But even though it was probably the dreariest decor he'd ever seen, the inside of the house was as clean and well-kept as the outside had been.

He decided he'd lock up behind him and stick her keys in the mailbox. He found a magnetic notepad stuck to the refrigerator and wrote her a message to that effect. He put it on the kitchen table and started to walk away when he noticed several envelopes and their contents scattered on the table. He saw utility bills, pay stubs, several credit card bills and a letter. He picked up the letter. It was from her landlord. She was a month behind.

He retrieved her purse from her bedroom, pulled out her

checkbook and flipped it open to see a balance of sixty-two dollars and seventeen cents.

He went to the kitchen and looked through the rest of the mail. A bill from a funeral home. A whopper. Fishing through a few more papers on the table, he found a program from the funeral of Margaret White, age sixty-two, who'd gone to meet her maker about three months ago. And judging from what he'd seen so far, she didn't have a father, either.

Growing nosier by the minute, he dug deeper and found a college catalog from the University of Texas at Austin. Several banking and finance courses were circled, but looking at her checkbook, she hadn't paid a dime for tuition for next semester. The course bulletin was a dream book, nothing more.

As he put the pieces of her life together, he started having second thoughts about her suitability as a wife. With her abysmal financial condition, would she really be so horrified at the prospect of a temporary marriage if he made it worth her while?

She might be the kind of woman who met her soul mate in the church choir, but after Cole divorced her in six months she'd still have the opportunity to find Mr. Right wherever she wanted to look. Daddy didn't appear to be around, so he wouldn't have to worry about turning a corner and finding himself looking down the barrel of a shotgun. She was a little on the plain side, which distressed him a bit, but kissing her hadn't been half bad. Maybe a woman who wasn't obsessed with her looks would be a pleasant change. For his own sanity he needed a halfway intelligent woman, and her college aspirations said she probably fit that description. And as far as college tuition was concerned, she'd probably jump at the twenty-five thousand dollars he was willing to give her for taking six months out of her life to become Mrs. Cole McCallum. And best of all, she was naive and innocent, which meant he'd be able to control the situation and call the shots. It just might work.

Cole smiled. It looked as if the good deed he'd done tonight had paid off, after all.

VIRGINIA BLINKED her eyes open and was met with early-morning sunlight filtering through her bedroom curtains. She lay motionless, a little disoriented. A few seconds later her senses woke up, and she let out a low, agonized groan.

A bass drum was playing inside her head, boom-boom-booming in sync with the rhythm of her heart. She tried to move, but every muscle ached, and when she swallowed her mouth was dry as parchment.

Then she felt something. A gentle tap on her shoulder. A pause. A harder tap.

A man's voice.

"Virginia. Time to get up."

Her eyes sprang open. She flipped over like a hotcake on a griddle and found herself staring directly into the eyes of Cole McCallum.

With a strangled scream, she pushed herself to a sitting position and backed against the headboard. She almost screamed again as she realized he was wearing nothing but a towel draped around his hips. His dark hair was damp and slicked back, and droplets of water clung to his shoulders.

"Wh-what are you doing?" Virginia sputtered.

"Thought I'd catch a quick shower. But don't worry. I left you plenty of hot water."

She couldn't think. She couldn't even breathe. But her eyes were in fine working order, roaming over Cole's body like those of a hungry diner checking out a smorgasbord. Her gaze traveled from his strong, sculpted shoulders, to his broad chest tapering down to a narrow waist, to a sharply defined set of abdominal muscles that made her think of a statue she'd once seen in an art-history book. She stared in awe at every inch of tanned skin, every ripple of muscle, every sexy bit of him that showed beyond the towel. For a split second her mind wandered to what lay beneath the towel and she wondered if it was perfection, too, then chastised herself for even thinking it.

Cole gave her a lazy smile. "I haven't had my body examined this closely since my last doctor's visit."

Virginia jerked her gaze away, feeling a hot blush rising on her cheeks. She'd just been surprised, that's all. That's why she'd stared. The man was clearly some kind of exhibitionist. Why else would he enjoy parading around nearly naked in front of a total stranger?

"I—I'd appreciate it if you'd put some clothes on."

He backed away a step or two, then turned and walked casually to a chair in the corner where his clothes lay.

"Better turn your back, sweetheart. I've been known to send a woman or two into shock."

Virginia turned away and focused on the ceramic butterfly music box on her nightstand, trying to keep her thoughts north of Cole's waist and south of his knees. Behind her she heard the faint thud of a damp bath towel hitting the hardwood floor. She told her heart to settle down, but it clearly intended to ignore her brain and beat her chest to death. She imagined him pulling his long, lean legs into those tight, faded jeans he'd worn last night, easing them up over his thighs and...and other things. Finally she heard a zipper, and she took a breath for the first time since she'd averted her eyes.

"All clear," he said a moment later, and she turned to see him shrugging into his shirt.

She peered at him tentatively. "Have you been here all night?"

That smile again. "I guess you don't remember, do you?"

Slowly the memories came together, like pieces of a jigsaw puzzle scattered about. Moving to music. Cole's arms wrapped around her. Her head on his shoulder. A long, incredible kiss...then another. And then...

And then the getting sick part. No wonder she felt so awful.

Then she remembered him saying something about key possession and drunk tanks and strip searches that was all a little fuzzy but retrievable, but as she played out the rest of the evening in her mind, panic set in. The last thing she remembered was being in Cole's car, driving home. Past that, she drew a blank. She glanced to the bed beside her and saw rumpled sheets and blankets.

She wasn't the only one who'd occupied it.

As she put two and two together and it started to look an awful lot like four, her heart shifted into overdrive. "Where did you sleep?"

He glanced at the bed beside her, then smiled. "You really *don't* remember, do you?"

She ducked her head, feeling that long-lost color returning to her cheeks. Could she actually have become a fallen woman and remembered nothing on the way down?

"Cole?" she said, barely able to croak out the words. "Did you...last night...?"

He buttoned one cuff, then started on the other. "Did I what?"

"You know..." She gestured toward the mussed blankets.

"Ah. You want to know if we made love." He shrugged. "Would it be a problem if we had?"

Oh, *God*. Virginia's hand flew to her mouth, and she squeezed her eyes closed. Every warning her mother had ever issued her came back in a huge rush of condemnation, and she thought she was going to be sick all over again.

A little music, a little fun and a lousy beer or two. That's all she'd wanted. Then, like some kind of naive fool, she'd allowed herself to fall into the hands of a man who practically made it a profession to rip the reputation out from under any girl he came in contact with. Embarrassment welled up inside her, then took a sharp turn toward anger.

"You—you had no right to do this!"

"No right to do what? As I recall, you were the one flashing cash around last night, looking for a good time."

"A kiss! That's all!"

"Now, didn't I tell you that sometimes you get a whole lot more than you bargained for?" He lifted an eyebrow and dropped his voice. "I'm one of those guys you don't mess with around closing time."

"But I wasn't of...of sound mind," she argued. "I'd had far too much to drink—"

"Whose fault was that?"

"And then...and then you dragged me home—"

"Saving you from driving drunk, if you'll remember."

"And then you did...did *this*," she went on, waving her hand wildly over the scrambled sheets and blankets. "And I didn't even *know* it!" She buried her head in her hands. She'd done it now. What had probably been heaven last night had bought her a one-way ticket for the other direction.

When she glanced up, his teasing smile had faded. "Is that what you really think, Virginia? That you passed out and I took advantage of you?"

"You were standing in my bedroom half-naked! What else am I to think?"

"Use some common sense, will you? You're wearing the same clothes you were wearing last night. I've undressed a lot of women in my life, but I can't say I've ever put any of their clothes back on."

She looked at herself and for the first time she realized that her blue jeans, horseshoe blouse and push-up bra were still intact. A little wrinkled here and there, but intact. Only her boots were missing.

"And where I come from," he went on, "we *always* undress when we take showers."

"You could have dressed in the bathroom!"

He gave her a cocky grin. "But that wouldn't have been nearly as much fun."

She glared at him, starting to get a little fed up with his attitude. He thought this was funny. She didn't see anything funny about it.

"Don't worry. Your virtue was safe last night. See, I've got this weird sexual preference. I prefer my women conscious."

She had to admit he was probably telling her the truth. If he'd made love to her, chances are she'd have remembered. Thinking about the way he kissed, she was pretty sure he could drag a woman out of a coma if he set his mind to it.

She closed her eyes, and for a brief moment she was back at that bar last night, standing under that neon beer sign with the music pulsing through her, and Cole was kissing her. She had no idea a simple kiss could feel like that, except that there was nothing simple about it. Sensations had bombarded her from all directions, turning her insides to mush and making her feel all dizzy and disoriented. She remembered the way Cole had smelled, that warm, musky, man smell she'd never experienced before because she'd never gotten close enough to a member of the opposite sex. She remembered that boneless, melting feeling that had taken over her body as he crushed her breathlessly against him, and the way he tasted when he slipped his tongue into her mouth and she found out firsthand what all the fuss was about French-kissing. Just thinking about it made her cheeks burn, and she turned away from him, knowing she was blushing. Just once in her life she wished she could keep her circulatory system from betraying every embarrassing thought she had, particularly where Cole was concerned.

She'd asked for a kiss, and he'd delivered. Boy, had he delivered. Thankfully, it appeared that was *all* he'd delivered. She sighed with relief, feeling as if her one-way trip to hell had just been canceled. When she finally got around to doing *that*, she swore it would be with a man she loved and a man who loved her, too, even if it took forever to find him. A man she was married to, for heaven's sake. She'd never make the same mistake her mother had. Never.

She inched her gaze around. "But if we didn't...I mean, if all we did is sleep, then what are you doing here?"

Cole sat on the chair and pulled his boots on, then stood. He sauntered to the bed where Virginia sat. He towered over her, and she had to tilt her head to meet his gaze.

"I have a proposition for you."

Virginia closed her eyes. "Oh, God."

"Take it easy, sweetheart. Not that kind of proposition." He sat on the bed next to her. She instinctively shrank away from him, and he slumped with frustration. "Are you *always* this uptight?"

"Yes! When I find a naked man in my bedroom who won't go away, yes! I get a little uptight!"

"Is that what you really want? For me to go away?"

"Yes!"

"Sorry. That's not an option." He checked his watch. "Look, Virginia, I'm a little short on time here, so I'm going to get right to the point. Listen up and try to follow, because I don't want to have to explain it twice. My grandmother died six months ago. She had a ranch about fifteen miles south of Coldwater that she willed to me, but she attached a few conditions. Part of the deal is that I have to be married and live on the ranch for six months before I get the deed, because she had this crazy idea that I needed to get married and settle down. Are you following me?"

Virginia's brain still felt fuzzy. "Yeah. I think so."

"Living on the ranch for six months is no problem. It's the other thing. The marriage thing."

She stared at him blankly.

"If I'm going to inherit that property, I need a wife, and I need one now."

He took a deep breath, then rubbed his hand across his mouth as if he'd give anything to hold back the words that were getting ready to come out.

"What I'm trying to say is...will you marry me?"

had this crazy idea that I needed to get married and settle down. Are you following me?"

Virginia's brain still felt fuzzy. "Yeah. I think so."

"Living on the ranch for six months is no problem. It's the other thing. The marriage."

She stared at him blankly.

"I've got to inherit that ranch," Cole said. "It means everything to me. But in order to do that, I have to get married."

"Why?"

"Long story. So I need a wife. Temporarily."

"So you're saying that you want me to—"

What was he trying to say, anyway?

4

THE MOMENT Cole said the word *marry*, whatever fuzziness Virginia still felt from her encounter with three bottles of beer last night was knocked right out of her. She sat up suddenly, staring at him with utter disbelief.

"*What* did you say?"

"It'll be a business arrangement. That's all. None of this till death do us part stuff. We stay on the ranch six months, I get the deed, then we get a divorce. That's it."

It was as if Cole were speaking a foreign language. The words themselves came through clearly, but she was having a really hard time comprehending them.

"And there's something in this deal for you, too," Cole went on. "Good thing, considering how broke you are."

Virginia's brain went on red alert. How did he know that? "Broke?" she said, trying to sound nonchalant. "I'm not broke."

"Your bank balance is approximately sixty-seven dollars. You've got bills up to your eyeballs and a landlord breathing down your neck. And I don't see you getting out anytime soon on that lousy salary they pay you at the bank."

"How do you know—?"

He gave her a knowing look, and all at once she thought about the stuff on her kitchen table, the bills, her check stubs. And then there was her purse. He'd already helped himself to that at the bar. Apparently he didn't think twice about rummaging through it again, and the thought of it infuriated her.

"You went through my things? While I was in here passed out, you looked through my whole house?"

"Not the whole house. I'm still not sure whether you wear briefs or bikinis."

Virginia gasped even as her face reddened with embarrassment. "Get out!"

Cole didn't budge.

"Get out of my house! Now!"

He regarded her for a long time, his dark eyes grim and calculating. Finally he held up his palms in resignation.

"Sure, sweetheart. Whatever you say."

He got up from the bed and headed for the door. "But it might be a long time before someone else offers you a way you can pay off all your bills and have enough money left over for college." He gave her a shrewd little smile. "See you around, Virginia."

He left the room, closing the door behind him with a gentle click.

Bills paid? College tuition?

She scrambled out of bed, yanked the bedroom door open and raced to the living room. "Cole. Wait."

He stopped and turned around. *Very* slowly.

"Tell me the part about the college tuition again."

Ten minutes later, she thought she'd absorbed it all. They would live on the ranch as man and wife for six months. After Cole took title to the ranch, they would get a divorce, and he would pay her twenty-five thousand dollars for her trouble. And during that time, since they'd be living on the ranch, she could bank most of her salary and pay off her bills, then at the end of six months she could be on the road to Austin. It was June right now. By December it would all be over with.

Simple as that.

Virginia slumped on the sofa, feeling overwhelmed. There was nothing simple about it.

"There are a dozen women in this town who would marry you. Why me?"

"To tell you the truth, I'm a little short on time, and you kind of fell into my lap."

That stung a little, but then again, he was asking for a business arrangement, not a real relationship. If Cole McCallum was looking for love, he'd be looking in another place. That made her heart sink a little, until she thought about the money she'd have after six months if she saved all her salary, then tossed twenty-five thousand dollars on top of it. Plenty of money to move to Austin, to go to college, to start a new life.

"What will happen to the ranch if you don't inherit it?" she asked.

"It'll go to Ben Murphy, my grandmother's second husband. But he's got more money than Midas. He doesn't need the ranch. He doesn't even want it. But he'll sure keep me from inheriting it if I don't meet the terms of the will."

"Why doesn't he want you to have it?"

"Let's just say that we've never seen eye to eye about anything."

"Why didn't your grandmother just will it to you without all the conditions?"

"It's like I said. She thinks I ought to get married and settle down. This is her way of trying to make that happen."

"But you don't want to settle down."

"Nope."

"So what will you do with the ranch once you have it?"

"Sell it."

"Sell it? Even though your grandmother wanted you to—"

"My motives are my own business, and I don't want you questioning them. All you have to do is decide whether or not you want that twenty-five thousand dollars."

Of course she wanted it. Right about now, there wasn't

much she wouldn't do to get money for college so she could leave Coldwater behind for good.

"Of course, I'll want you to sign a prenuptial agreement," Cole said, "which basically states that you get nothing but the twenty-five thousand dollars when we divorce. I've already had a lawyer draw up divorce papers, which we'll both sign, and when the six months is up, I'll execute them and we'll go our separate ways."

Virginia felt her head spinning as she tried to absorb it all. Ultimately, though, the part she understood the best was the part about the twenty-five thousand dollars.

She looked around the house, at the four walls she'd stared at since she was old enough to remember. Life with her mother had been one sermon after another, which she put on hold only long enough to complain about her various aches and pains. Virginia could still hear her mother calling to her from her bedroom, tugging on that invisible cord of neediness she'd wound around her daughter to keep her drowning in guilt. She'd forced responsibility on her that no person her age should ever have had to deal with, and it wasn't until her mother's sudden heart attack and subsequent death that Virginia had truly understood the prison she'd been in—a prison she was now desperate to break out of.

But could she actually go through with it? Could she marry a man she didn't even know? And above all, could she spend six months in the same house as Cole McCallum?

"So do we have a deal?" Cole said.

"No! I mean, I have to think about it. I can't just jump right into something like this."

"Sorry. There's no time for you to think about it. It's now or never."

"No," she said, shaking her head. "Really. This is crazy. I just don't think—"

"Come on, Ginny. Lighten up, will you? This arrangement will be good for both of us."

Virginia's heart skipped. "What did you say?"

"I said the arrangement will be—"

"No. What did you call me?"

"Ginny?"

She stared at him.

"That is your nickname, isn't it? Short for Virginia?"

"Uh, yeah."

Not once in her life had anyone called her anything but Virginia. Her mother certainly never had, or her teachers, or even the people she worked with. She was Virginia—uptight, boring Virginia who didn't even warrant a casual nickname. Hearing Ginny come out of Cole's mouth right now gave her a feeling she'd never had before, as if there was another flesh-and-blood person hiding inside her, dying to get out. One named Ginny who said yes far more than she said no, who took chances, who looked adventure and excitement right in the face and never blinked.

"I'll do it," she said.

"You will?"

"Yes. I will."

She stiffened for a moment, not completely sure those words had come out of her mouth. Had she actually said she'd marry Cole McCallum? Suddenly she felt a little woozy, as if she were going to keel right over.

She took a deep, calming breath. It was going to be okay. She could do this. After all, she had a little time to get used to the idea, to reconcile herself to the fact that while she'd be married to Cole, it was really just a business deal, and business deals were nothing to get in a tizzy about. It would take a few days at least to get a blood test and a marriage license, and by that time—

"Ginny," Cole said. "One more thing. About the wedding."

"Yes?"

"I have to be a married man by tonight."

Ginny gaped at him. "Tonight?"

"Pack your bags, sweetheart. We're going to Vegas."

THE LAS VEGAS strip after dark was a sight Ginny had never expected to see—a whirlpool of multicolored lights so bright that it looked as if the sun hadn't bothered to set. Everything seemed fluid and full of motion, cars gliding down the street and people moving along the sidewalk in a never-ending swirl of activity, so bright and glitzy that it made the Lone Wolf Saloon look like a church parish hall.

Cole had rented a car at the airport and now, only a few hours after leaving Dallas, they were driving down Las Vegas Boulevard. They'd already stopped to get a marriage license at the Clark County Courthouse, which to Ginny's utter surprise was open until midnight.

In the trunk of the car was her overnight bag, a twenty-year-old brown-vinyl creation that had belonged to her mother. It held her nightgown, her toothbrush and all her other toiletries, as well as a change of clothes for tomorrow. According to Cole, there were no return flights to Dallas tonight, so they'd have to stay here, then fly back first thing in the morning.

Flying. What an experience *that* had been.

Feeling that plane swooshing a hundred miles an hour down the runway had left her positively breathless, and it wasn't until they'd been in the air for several minutes that Cole had managed to pry her fingernails out of his arm. She didn't feel much more comfortable right now, having that same kind of swoopy sensation in her stomach, only for a totally different reason.

Cole continued on Las Vegas Boulevard, where one chapel after another, with names like L'Amour Chapel, Chapel of the Flowers and Viva Las Vegas, lined the street. She looked longingly at those that actually looked like chapels, white clapboard structures with flowers and nice shrubs out front and a minimum of neon lights.

Unfortunately, Cole drove right past those and pulled into the parking lot of one of the most garish buildings Ginny had ever seen. It took her a moment to accept the fact that it was their destination and another moment to convince herself not to fling open the car door and run screaming into the night.

The building was painted a deep rosy pink, with red shuttered windows and an arch of golden neon bulbs outlining the front door. A pair of six-foot-tall wooden cutout cupids guarded the entrance with their little bows and arrows poised for attack. Even with the car windows closed, she could hear an outdoor speaker blaring, "I Love You Truly." And the sign out front, illuminated with three gigantic floodlights, read Cupid's Little Chapel of Love.

Ginny couldn't believe her eyes. She stared dumbly, words escaping her completely.

Cole glanced at her, then killed the car engine. "It was the only one with a Saturday night appointment left."

"Oh," Ginny said. Just oh. What else *could* she say?

"This is strictly business, Ginny," he said. "Remember that."

Thank God it was only business. If this were the place where she was going to have a wedding for real, she'd have her face in her hands right now, sobbing uncontrollably. She hoped it would be better on the inside.

No such luck.

The reception area was draped in huge swaths of cheap red-and-pink fabric, with benches upholstered in something that looked like red velveteen. And cupids were everywhere.

There were pictures of cupids on the walls. Cupid figurines on the reception counter. Cupids flying in formation on the border paper at the ceiling. It looked like a huge, gaudy Valentine's Day card somebody would send as a practical joke.

Cole motioned for her to sit down on a bench while he went to the reception desk to confirm their reservation, then returned to sit next to her. She squeezed over to give him room, which put her almost thigh-to-thigh with the guy sitting next to her, though she doubted he realized it. His attention seemed to be focused on the flamboyant redhead in his lap. Her arms were looped around his neck, and they were smooching and giggling, totally oblivious to the other people in the room.

Across from them sat a petite little blonde and a painfully thin guy with long, dark hair. Neither of them looked a day over twenty. She looked pregnant. He looked panic-stricken. Another couple sat next to them wearing shorts and T-shirts, looking as if they were waiting in line for a ride at Disney World.

Then Ginny wondered, *What do I look like to them?*

She'd worn her navy blue dress with the lace collar, because somehow she felt that no matter what the reason she was getting married, she really ought to look her best. Cole, on the other hand, wore a pair of jeans, a denim shirt and boots. If they hadn't been sitting right next to each other, not a soul would have taken them for a couple.

Approximately every ten minutes, a couple would leave the chapel, and a short, stout woman whose name tag read Myrna would come out to the reception area and call another name. The couple sitting next to Ginny tied the knot, then stumbled out the door. So did the pregnant couple. Then the Disney World people went in, and Ginny felt a tremor of panic.

It's not a real wedding, she kept telling herself. *It's just pretend.*

Several minutes passed. Then the chapel door opened, the Disney World people left, and Myrna called Cole's name.

Ginny rose and walked with Cole into the chapel, where she saw that the cupid theme wasn't confined to the reception area. A man stood at the back of the room in a shiny brown suit and narrow tie, his wispy gray hair falling in skinny strings over his ears. Another man stood to one side, armed with an assortment of cameras. Myrna consulted her clipboard.

"Okay, let's see what we're doing here," she said, running her fingertip down the page. Then a startled look came over her face. "There seems to be a mistake."

"Mistake?" Cole said.

"Yes. It says here you're not purchasing a video. Not even any photos. Is that correct?"

"That's correct."

Her gaze slid farther down the page, her expression growing progressively more distressed. "Champagne flutes—no. Picture postcards—no. His-and-hers commemorative T-shirts—no." Her gaze panned to Cole, her brow furrowed accusingly. "Do you mean to tell me you're not even going to buy a fresh-flower bouquet for your fiancée?"

"Is there a problem with that?" Cole said.

Myrna turned her gaze to Ginny. Ginny shrugged helplessly.

The woman pursed her lips with displeasure, eyeing Cole as if he were the most vile creature who'd ever slithered into Cupid's Little Chapel of Love. She set her clipboard down, then grabbed a tattered bouquet of silk flowers off a chair and handed it to Ginny with a sympathetic smile. "Here, sweetie. You take this. It's on the house." Then she turned and shot

Cole a look so nasty Ginny was surprised he didn't turn to stone.

Then Myrna leaned in close to Ginny, dropping her voice. "You sure about this?"

No. She wasn't the least bit sure about it, but she'd come too far to turn back now.

"It's okay," she told Myrna. "Really. We're just on a tight budget, that's all. My fiancé is very...thrifty."

"Thrifty's one thing," Myrna whispered. "Being a tight-wad's another."

"Can we get on with it?" Cole said.

Myrna put her fists on her hips and glared at him. "You in some kinda hurry or what?"

"Lady, if we weren't in a hurry, would we be in Vegas?"

Myrna sniffed with disgust, then turned to Ginny. "You haven't said 'I do' yet. There's still plenty of time to say you don't."

"Hey!" Cole said. "Are you in the business of marrying people, or breaking them up?"

The man in the ugly brown suit let out a long-suffering sigh. "Myrna, honey, this is the third one you've gotten in the middle of tonight. If we're gonna make the bills this month, you might want to think about letting this one go."

"But, Henry—"

"If they're meant for each other, fine. If they're not, another lawyer makes a killing. Either way, it's none of our business. Now, start the music."

Myrna tossed Cole one last sneer, then turned to her husband with a dismissive wave of her hand. "Fine," she muttered. "Guess I can't save 'em all. Make it permanent, Henry."

Permanent. If only the woman knew.

Myrna fired up the music, and Henry started the ceremony. Through it all, Ginny felt Myrna's eyes on her, the all-knowing eyes of a woman who could spot a love match at fifty paces and knew for a fact that this wasn't one of them. Ginny tried to ignore her, concentrating instead on Henry's words, but soon his voice became nothing more than a droning buzz.

Then he got to the part about the ring, and when Ginny realized Cole didn't have one, she furtively yanked the ring off the fourth finger of her right hand, a gold one with three diamond chips she'd gotten as a bonus gift for opening a new account at the bank. She slipped it into Cole's hand. He looked totally fed up with the whole thing.

So did Myrna.

He put the ring on her left hand and mumbled the appropriate words. Henry asked for their "I do's." They complied, and he pronounced them man and wife.

Ginny realized she'd been holding her breath and she let it out in one long, silent exhalation. Okay, that hadn't been so bad. She'd expected to feel different somehow, but she didn't. She supposed it was because she wasn't really married, not in the true sense of the word. It was just a business deal. Nothing soul-searching or earth-shattering. Nothing at all to get excited about. Nothing—

"You may kiss the bride," Henry said.

Her heart nearly stopped. How could she have forgotten about this part?

She turned to Cole, wondering what he had in mind. If the look on his face meant anything, kissing wasn't it. But Myrna was giving him that chastising look again, tap-tap-tapping her toe, so he finally gave up and placed a dry, perfunctory kiss on her lips.

Myrna's stout little body heaved with disgust. She looked at Henry and shook her head sadly.

Henry peeked over the top of his bifocals. "Boy, unless

you're planning on sleeping alone tonight, you'd best get to kissin' like you mean it."

Cole glared at the proprietors of Cupid's Little Chapel of Love for a good five seconds, then finally spat out a breath of resignation.

"Aw, what the hell."

He took hold of Ginny's arm, pulled her against him, then swept her backward and dropped his mouth down on hers. Every bit of the passion that had been absent from their wedding ceremony exploded in a kiss so hot that she was afraid Cupid's Little Chapel of Love was going to spontaneously combust.

She heard a gasp of shock from Myrna and a sound that just might have been Henry's jaw hitting the floor. But all she could do was lie back in Cole's arms, helpless as a rag doll, clutching his shoulders blindly as his mouth consumed hers. If the kiss he'd given her last night was a hundred dollars' worth, she was going to have to win the lottery to pay for this one. Of course, he was doing it only as a backlash against Myrna's extreme displeasure with him, but that didn't mean she couldn't enjoy it just the same.

After kissing her for what seemed like forever, Cole slowly brought her back to her feet. Once they had a few quick signatures on the marriage license, he swept her out the door. Ginny glanced over her shoulder to see Myrna's face fixed in a mask of total disbelief, and she thought she heard Myrna say something to Henry about how flowers were one thing, but a man who could kiss like that was something else entirely, and maybe Ginny knew what she was doing after all.

COLE THOUGHT the brain-dead night clerk at the Paradise Hotel was never going to get them the key to their room. Ginny had excused herself to go to the ladies' room while he registered, leaving him standing there tapping his fingertips on the desk, obsessed with one thought only. Getting on with the honeymoon. And it had started the moment he'd kissed her.

Up to that point, he'd been thinking of nothing but getting the ceremony over with, especially when it appeared as if Ma and Pa Kettle were going to drag it on forever. Consequently, he hadn't spent a lot of time thinking about what came after their "I do's." But the minute he'd laid his lips on Ginny's again, he remembered how soft and sweet she'd felt last night, melting in his arms, getting her first taste of kissing and loving it.

Tonight he could give her a taste of something else.

Finally the clerk gave him the key. He intercepted Ginny coming from the ladies' room and headed for an open elevator. As they ascended, he was consumed with the thought of seeing what was underneath that pristine little dress she was wearing. Not that he expected any big surprises. She would be wearing white cotton panties with a matching bra that had one of those little pink roses at the cleavage, and he couldn't imagine anything less provocative. But he could remove both those things in short order, right after he took her hair down from that prissy little barrette and peeled her dress right off her.

He was crazy even to think it, of course. She'd gone nuts at the very idea that they might have had sex last night. What would she say about doing it tonight?

Then again, they were married now. Women like Ginny undoubtedly put great stock in such things, requiring pieces of paper with official signatures before they did something as fun and meaningless as have sex. Well, they were married. He had that piece of paper to prove it. So what was to stop them?

Absolutely nothing.

A moment later they stepped off the elevator and headed

down the hall to room 2413. He unlocked the door and swung it open, motioning for her to enter.

"Oh!" she said as she walked in, turning around, her face filled with wonder. "Look at this room!"

Actually, the decor was fairly modest, with a navy-and-gold floral bedspread, navy drapes tied back with gold sashes and dark walnut furniture. Only one weak lamp illuminated the room, which helped mask the fact that the place could use a good coat of paint. Still, Ginny seemed thrilled with it. Given the house where she lived, he figured anything the least bit upscale would look good to her.

With her overnight bag and her purse still draped over her shoulder, she hurried to the window. She opened the drapes and looked down twenty-four stories to the street below.

"Oh! Look at all the lights! I can't believe how beautiful it is!"

Cole clicked the door shut.

Ginny spun around. She stared at him, first with surprise, then with confusion. Then her gaze circled the room, finally coming to rest on the king-size bed. She looked at Cole, and even at the distance between them, he saw her swallow hard, staring at him like a scared rabbit.

He smiled to himself. In a matter of a few minutes, he would have all that doubt kissed right out of her, and before she knew it, she would be naked in his bed. And he would make sure she didn't regret it. He didn't remember a time in his life when a woman had left his bed unhappy, and he didn't intend to have her be the first. Tomorrow morning when they woke up, she would be right there for him again. And when they got home to Coldwater, she would be there for him every single day, and it surprised him just how appealing the thought of that was. He never would have imagined it, but there was definitely something to be said for being a married man.

With a casual sweep of his arm he tossed his suitcase onto the floor, then started toward her.

5

GINNY STOOD with her back to the window, staring at Cole in the dim light of the hotel room. Something about the look on his face sent shivers of apprehension shooting up her spine, and her heart leaped into a quick, erratic rhythm.

"Wh-what's the matter?" she asked.

"Nothing's the matter," he murmured, his voice silky smooth and hot as sin. "Absolutely nothing."

He moved across the room, closing the space between them in measured increments, his eyes fixed on hers in an unwavering stare.

"Wh-where's your room?" she asked him.

"My room?" He laughed softly. "You're standing in it."

"Oh. Then...where's my room?"

"You're standing in it."

"Cole?"

"Yes?"

"There's only one bed in this room."

"That's right."

"Why didn't you get two rooms?"

"Waste of money. We're married."

"But—"

"We slept together last night."

"Yes, I know, but—"

He stopped in front of her. She took a step backward and bumped into the window, staring at him. He put his hand on the window near her right ear and leaned in closer still.

"What are you doing?" she asked.

"What do you think I'm doing?"

"I...don't know."

He teased his fingertip along her neck just above the collar of her dress. "Don't you?"

For a full five seconds, Ginny stopped breathing. She felt as if she'd gotten struck by lightning and it had zapped all her muscle strength. He didn't mean...he couldn't mean...

"You...you said this was a business arrangement."

"Haven't you ever heard of mixing business with pleasure?"

He leaned in to kiss her. She recoiled sharply to one side, placing her palms against his chest. "Wait a minute. You never said anything about wanting to do...this."

"You never said anything about *not* wanting to do...this."

"But we're not really married."

"I have a license that says we are."

"But I never thought—"

He took her purse off her shoulder and tossed it aside.

"We never talked about—"

He grabbed her overnight bag and tossed it next to her purse.

"I was sure you understood—"

He reached around her neck with both hands, and her heart nearly stopped. He unclasped the barrette holding her hair at the nape of her neck, tossed it onto the dresser, then spread her hair on her shoulders. He picked up a handful, letting it spill through his fingers and fall in ripples against her lace collar. He inched closer, so close she felt his body heat, and an unfamiliar physical awareness swept over her that was scary and mysterious and exciting all at the same time.

"You have beautiful hair," he whispered.

Ginny felt a jolt of pure exhilaration. It was the first time in her life that somebody had used the word *beautiful* in reference to any part of her. His words thrilled her, but at the same time they were totally unreal. She wasn't beautiful. Not in any way. So why was he telling her that?

Because he wanted… Oh, *God*.

Ginny's knees buckled a little, and she consciously had to lock them to keep herself upright. Cole took her face in his hands and stared at her. His touch electrified her. Terrified her. Made her want to pull him closer at the same time she was desperate to push him away because the sensory overload was almost unbearable.

"You'll enjoy it," he whispered against her lips. "I promise you. I'll make it so good for you you'll want to do it again and again…" He brushed his lips against hers. "And again."

Then he kissed her, a kiss so deliciously deep and breathtaking that she practically fainted from the feeling. It was slower, more languid than the other kisses he'd given her, as if he had all night to explore her mouth with his. But while Cole was doing his best to warm up any part of her body he touched, something deep inside her remained cold.

He didn't want her. He wanted any woman whom he'd been able to convince to marry him. If it hadn't been her, it would have been somebody else. She had no meaning to him at all.

If only he'd been content to kiss her forever, she'd have given him carte blanche. But he clearly wanted more. More of something she had no idea how to give him. More of something she had no *business* giving him.

Still kissing her deeply, he slid his hands to her hips. He pulled her against him, and her heart skipped a beat when she realized what it was he'd pulled her against. He wound his left hand around the small of her back, then skimmed his right hand along her ribs. She felt mounting anticipation as his hand eased closer to her breast, and when he finally circled it with his hand and squeezed it softly, she let out a breathy gasp and tried to pull away.

"Cole. Don't. Please don't."

Still he held on to her, waiting patiently until she stilled against him. Then he laid his palm along her neck, his thumb grazing her cheek. "It's okay, sweetheart. I know you've never done this before. You're probably just a little scared."

No, actually, she was a *lot* scared, but that was beside the point. She'd dreamed about sex since she was old enough to know there were people doing it and she wasn't. But it wasn't actually sex she'd dreamed about. She'd dreamed about making love. With a man who loved her. When Cole touched her, it excited her in ways she never knew she could be excited. When she looked into his eyes, though, she saw a void, something missing, something essential that went deep to the heart of a woman when a man looked at her, something that for all her inexperience she knew should be there. It wasn't.

"I asked you to stop," she said.

"Relax," he whispered, touching his lips to her neck, her cheek. "It'll be—"

"I said *no!*"

He pulled away with a startled expression. Almost immediately, his surprise gave way to something that looked a lot like anger, and all at once she realized she didn't know a thing about the man she'd just traveled a thousand miles with. The man she'd married. The man who just might insist she fulfill her wifely duties even though she'd never even been touched by a man until last night, and the thought of that scared her to death.

"Please don't force me to do this," she whispered.

Cole physically recoiled, his eyes wide with astonishment. "Force you? Is that what you think? That I would *force* you?"

"I—I don't really know you, Cole. So I don't know what you'd do."

His jaw tightened with anger. "I've never forced a woman to do *anything* she didn't want to do, and I sure as hell don't intend to start now. If you don't want to have sex, fine. But trust me when I tell you, sweetheart—it's your loss!"

He turned and stormed into the bathroom, shutting the door behind him with a solid thunk.

Ginny looked around helplessly. The room was suddenly so quiet, echoing the lost, lonely feeling welling inside her. She was in a Las Vegas hotel room a thousand miles from home, married to a man she barely knew, a man who right now wasn't happy with her in the least.

She sat on the bed, and all at once her mother started talking again, in that uncanny beyond-the-grave way she had that made it seem as if she were still alive, standing over her, berating her within an inch of her life.

Are you out of your mind? You're in Sin City with a man who's only using you to get what he wants. What kind of a fool are you, anyway?

Ginny squeezed her eyes closed, wondering how she could have gotten herself into this mess. It appeared that everything her mother had ever told her about men was absolutely true. Cole thought just because they were legally married, he was free to take advantage of her any way he wanted to.

She sat up straighter, feeling a new sense of resolve. She decided right then that he wasn't entitled to anything just because he had her name on a marriage license. He could only take advantage of her if she let him.

And she wasn't going to let him.

COLE TURNED the shower on full blast and ducked under it, letting the water beat down on him, hoping it might help ease his frustration. It didn't.

It's your loss.

Yeah, right. Her loss? She couldn't have cared less. He was the one still feeling as if he were about to explode.

That had been an incredibly stupid thing to say, but he'd been so astonished that she'd turned him down he'd barely known *what* to say. After all, hadn't she begged him to kiss her at the Lone Wolf last night?

He ran the bar of soap over his body, scrubbing with an intensity that just about peeled his skin off. Technically they were married. Weren't there laws about this kind of thing? Didn't a woman *have* to have sex with her husband?

He sighed. No. Of course she didn't. This was twenty-first-century America. But damned if he didn't feel like calling his congressman to see how fast he could resurrect a few of those archaic laws and get them back on the books.

By the time he turned off the water and stepped out of the shower, he was starting to feel a little guilty. She was so innocent, and he'd come on way too strong, pushing her to do something she wasn't the least bit ready for.

He slicked his hands through his hair, then grabbed a towel and dried off, telling himself to calm down. Yes, she was his wife, but it might take a little while for her to be comfortable with that. The last thing he wanted was a woman in his bed who didn't want to be there.

Calm and cool. That's what he needed to be.

He came out of the bathroom, a towel wrapped around his hips, and headed for his suitcase. Ginny was sitting on the bed, still wearing that immaculate little dress, looking as if she were parked front row center in church listening to a particularly scathing sermon. She didn't turn around.

"Cole?" she said, staring at the dresser.

He pulled a pair of sweatpants out of his suitcase. "Yeah?"

"I don't want you ever to do that again."

"Do what?"

"K-kiss me." She picked up her skirt and twisted it nervously between her fingers. "And other things. Our contract says nothing about me being required to...submit to that."

All Cole's resolve to remain calm and cool flew right out the window. *Submit* to that? As if he were asking her to take a beating?

"Promise me, Cole. For the next six months, promise me you won't—"

"No. I'm not promising any such thing!"

"You have to. Right now. If you don't, I'll..." She squeezed her skirt so hard that her knuckles whitened.

"You'll what?"

She raised her chin, and even five paces away he could see it quivering. "I'll have our marriage annulled."

Annulled? *Annulled?*

He thought he'd foreseen all the potential problems of marrying this woman, but not once in his most pessimistic moment had he expected to face an obstacle like this.

"Actually, Ginny, you can't do that. Our contract states that you're not allowed to divorce me for six months."

"Yes, but it says nothing about annulment."

Cole had no idea if such a challenge would hold up in court or not, but he sure as hell didn't need that kind of complication when so much was riding on the outcome.

"Are you sure about this, Ginny? You don't want sex?"

She bowed her head and stared at her lap. "That's right."

"Not now, or not ever?"

"Not ever." She paused. "Well, eventually, I suppose. With the man I marry."

"We *are* married."

"Yes, we are. Contractually speaking. But—"

"Would you forget about the damned contract for a minute? Sex with your husband is not a sin!"

"I never said it was. When I have a real husband, things will be different."

Cole wanted to scream. He'd never thought for one second that he'd be on the verge of begging his *wife* to have sex with him. It was downright humiliating.

"Fine," he said. "I won't touch you. Any particular distance I have to stay away from you?"

"No. Just don't...do what you did tonight."

"I wouldn't think of it."

"Good. That's...good."

For the first time she turned to face him, then immediately averted her eyes. "Cole, *please* put some clothes on!"

"I don't think I'm obligated to do that, Ginny. Contractually speaking."

"If you don't—"

"What? You'll get an annulment? Are there any other rules you'd care to make?"

"I don't think simple modesty is too much to ask."

Any other woman would be tearing his clothes off him right about now, and the fact that Ginny wanted him to put his clothes *on*, and on their wedding night, no less, was just about more than he could tolerate.

"Fine," he said. While her back was still turned, he pulled the towel loose from around his hips, hurled it to the floor, then yanked on his sweatpants. He grabbed the bedspread and whipped it aside.

"It's late," he told her. "I'm sleeping in this bed. If you want to join me, fine. If you don't, that's fine, too, but you'll have to make other arrangements yourself."

Ginny sighed. "Well, I suppose we've already occupied the same bed once. One more time couldn't hurt. And it's a large bed. As long as you stay on your side—"

"Should I draw a line down the middle?"

Ginny stared at him a moment, as if she were considering taking him up on that. "No. I'm sure that won't be necessary."

While Cole lay in bed, still fuming, she took her overnight bag into the bathroom. He heard tooth brushing, toilet flushing, water running. She emerged minutes later wearing a nightgown—a long pink creation that contained so damned much fabric he could barely see the top of her head or the tips of her toes. In his opinion, any woman Ginny's age ought to be draped in something short, black and slinky. Period. But when he tried to imagine her in sexy lingerie, the sight of all that fabric squelched any fantasy he tried to work up.

She slid beneath the covers on the other side of the bed, hugging the edge and taking up only a tiny ball of space, staying as far away from him as was physically possible. That really irritated him. He'd offered her a night of pleasure she would never forget, and here she was treating him as if she couldn't stand the thought of him touching her. She turned out the light, and after a few moments, her rhythmic breathing told him she'd fallen asleep.

He tucked his arm behind his head, suddenly wide awake. Fifteen minutes passed, then thirty. He found the more he tried to sleep, the more he thought about the warm, untried little body curled up next to him inside those yards and yards of flannel.

Damn, this was crazy. It was Ginny White on the other side of that bed, a plain, inexperienced little thing whom he wouldn't have looked twice at before last night, and now all he could think about was touching her.

He knew now that he'd come on too strong tonight, thinking he'd sweep her right off her feet, underestimating her fear of the unknown.

He wouldn't be making that mistake again.

6

COLE BARELY SPOKE to Ginny the whole way home on the plane and during the drive to Coldwater. Every minute seemed to stretch on endlessly, and soon her stomach had tied itself into knots of dread at what lay ahead. Ever since last night, when she'd insisted on the no-touching rule, Cole had extended it to include no talking, too.

Just because she'd insisted he not touch her, didn't mean she wasn't preoccupied with the thought of it approximately fifty-nine minutes out of every hour. In the close confines of the plane, occasionally their arms had brushed against each other. That was all it took for Ginny's thoughts to be dragged to last night, when she'd felt so hot and flushed from his kisses that she could barely speak to tell him never to do it again. No wonder her mother had warned her about men. Every time Cole kissed her it turned her brain to mush.

Before going to the ranch, she suggested he take her by her house to get her car and pick up some clothes to last her for a couple of days. She would decide later what to do with her house and the rest of her belongings. But Cole had been adamant about putting in an appearance at the ranch first and declaring it their official residence. According to his grandmother's will, this was the last day for them to move in, and he told Ginny he had no intention of Murphy catching him on a technicality.

As they drove through the front gates of the ranch, Ginny stared in awe at the huge turn-of-the-century prairie-style residence with its massive wraparound front porch, forest-green shutters and meticulous landscaping. It sat on a rise in the distance, postcard-picturesque against a canvas of blue sky mingling with the orange light of the evening sun. Her fears concerning living with Cole were instantly put to rest. In a house so large, their paths might not even have to cross.

"It's beautiful," she murmured.

"Yeah," Cole said. "It's beautiful, all right. Unfortunately, Murphy still lives there." He pointed down the road. "*That's* where we'll be living."

Ginny looked in the direction he pointed, and panic set in all over again.

It was a house. Barely. The plain little structure couldn't have been more than seven hundred square feet, whitewash dull with a light gray roof. A couple of window-unit air conditioners protruded from its sides. It was the kind of place that a few shrubs or flowers might have been able to brighten up, if only someone had bothered to plant any.

"It's the foreman's house. Nobody's used it in years. My grandmother specified in her will that I'd have to use it while I'm here."

"Oh," Ginny said, disappointment welling inside her. "It's very...cozy."

"That's one way of putting it."

Ginny looked past the house to the ranch land beyond it, which, unlike the house, was nothing but wide open space. Lush hills rolled majestically as far as she could see, with trees leafed in full summer splendor. Farther down the road stood a large barn with adjoining corrals that were filled with horses.

Ginny felt a rush of excitement. She'd wanted a horse since she was old enough to say the word, but of course, her mother had given her a lecture on the nebulous horrors that would befall a young girl who dared to sit astride such a wild, powerful beast. Ginny had come away thinking that maybe riding a horse was a sin, but she hadn't been completely certain.

"Do you think I can learn to ride a horse?" she asked Cole.

He looked toward the corrals, then shrugged. "If you want to. And if I know Murphy, he'll be happy to put you to work."

Ginny felt a rush of exhilaration at the prospect of even touching a horse, much less riding one. Then Cole pulled up in front of the foreman's house and they went inside, and the little bit of elation she'd felt was immediately forgotten.

What had looked small on the outside looked positively microscopic on the inside, with sparse, utilitarian furnishings, wood floors and bare walls. It was neat and tidy, but musty-smelling from being closed up. She took the ten-second tour and realized there was a much bigger problem than she'd anticipated.

It had only one bedroom.

Did Cole actually expect her to share a bed with him for the next six months? For a moment she felt faint. She wasn't good at telling him no. If she had to do it every night, sooner or later something was going to happen between them that she was sure she was going to regret.

She met him in the living room, and all at once he seemed more big and imposing and *sexy* than he ever had before.

"Cole?"

"Yes?"

"You knew this was a one-bedroom house," she said.

"Yes. I did."

"Why didn't you tell me?"

"Would it have mattered if I had?"

"Yes! This house is tiny! With both of us living here—"

He held up his palm. "All right, Ginny. All right. I'll sleep on the sofa. You can have the bedroom. Does that make you feel better?"

She felt somewhat relieved, but still there was only one bathroom, one bedroom closet, one dresser...

Nothing was going to be easy about this deal they'd made. Absolutely nothing. But then again, she could accommodate a lot of inconvenience for twenty-five thousand dollars, couldn't she?

She sighed with resignation. "I suppose it'll be okay, as long as you respect my privacy."

"You might as well kiss the privacy thing goodbye right now. You're going to have to lighten up a little if we're going to make this work."

"No. The only way to make this work is to plan ahead. First of all, I realize it's not fair for you to have to sleep on the sofa the whole time. We can take turns. And we can set up a schedule for the bathroom, and as far as cooking—"

All at once she heard a car engine out front. "Who's that?"

Cole glanced out the window. "Looks like Murphy saw us drive in."

They stepped onto the front porch, and Ginny watched as an older man got out of a shiny red pickup truck and walked slowly to the porch steps. He stopped, staring up at them, a hat shading his craggy face. A toothpick protruded from the corner of his mouth, a mouth that seemed to be set in a permanent frown.

"I see you made it," he said to Cole, then checked his watch. "With a whole six hours to spare."

Cole returned the man's deadpan stare. "Murphy, this is my wife, Ginny. Ginny, Ben Murphy. My grandmother's husband."

Ginny stepped forward a little, wondering if maybe she should shake his hand or something. Then she got closer and saw just how frigid his expression was. He clearly wasn't interested in social niceties, so she kept her hands to herself.

"So tell me," Murphy said, directing his question at Cole. "Just how long have you and the missus been married?"

Cole folded his arms across his chest. "Seventeen hours."

"I expected as much."

"My grandmother's will is very clear—"

"Your grandmother's will," Murphy said sharply, "is a product of wishful thinking. Nothing more."

Cole had told Ginny they'd never seen eye to eye. That had apparently been the understatement of the century.

Murphy turned to Ginny, and she seriously wished she could crawl under the porch to avoid his penetrating gaze.

"I know you, don't I?" he asked.

"No, I don't think—"

"You're a teller at the bank."

Suddenly Ginny felt transparent as a newly washed window. "Yes."

"You seem like a nice girl. Not exactly the kind I expected him to show up with."

"We're married," Cole said. "That's all that matters."

"I assume you've got a license to back that up."

"Yes, I do. Care to see it?"

"No need. I figured you'd have all the paperwork in order."

"I assume you're as good as your word," Cole said. "If I fulfill the letter of the law where the will is concerned, I'll get the deed."

"Yeah. But if you think I'm going to make this easy for you, you've got another think coming."

Cole just stared at him.

"And remember what I told you before. The provisions of the will are just between you and me." He paused, eyeing Ginny. "And now, I suppose, your *wife*."

He said the word with such flagrant distaste that even in the warmth of the early-June evening, Ginny shivered. Then he turned to Cole.

"I won't have your manipulation of this situation make Edna look like a fool," Murphy went on. "You're going to tell people you've come back to the ranch to go into partnership with me. When the end of the six months comes—assuming you fulfill the requirements of Edna's will—we'll simply say I'm retiring and you're taking it over permanently. It's nobody's business to know anything more than that."

Cole's only reaction was a slight tightening of his jaw, but it was pretty clear he wasn't taking Murphy's attitude kindly. Likewise, Ginny could tell Murphy probably had a pretty good idea about what Cole intended to do with the ranch once he had the title.

"We've got a busy day tomorrow," Murphy said. "Be at the barn at eight in the morning."

He got into his truck and started the engine, then put it into reverse, swung it around a hundred and eighty degrees and headed up the road toward the ranch house on the hill. Cole's expression was stony and emotionless.

All at once Ginny felt ashamed for what they were doing. It was legal. But was it right? And why hadn't she really stopped to ponder that before now?

"Maybe we shouldn't have done this," she murmured.

"Don't pay any attention to him, Ginny. It's me he's mad at, not you."

"No, actually it appears that he doesn't think much of either of us."

There was a long, uncomfortable silence. Cole stared straight ahead, watching as Murphy's truck headed up the gravel road toward the main house.

"What happened between you two?" Ginny asked. "Why doesn't he like you?"

"It doesn't matter. All that matters is that my grandmother wanted me to have the ranch, and as long as I technically fulfill the provisions of her will, there's nothing he can say about it."

"But I don't think she really intended—"

"Stop it, Ginny. We have a deal. We're in this together for six months, so you'd better start getting used to it."

She opened her mouth to object, only to realize he was right. Maybe she should have asked a lot more questions before agreeing to this deal, but the decision was made. Now she was going to have to live with it.

"Here's our story," Cole said. "We saw each other on Friday night at the Lone Wolf and remembered each other from high school. After spending the next twenty-four hours together, we decided to head to Vegas to get married."

"Do you really think anyone will believe that?"

"People do impulsive things all the time. That's why Las Vegas has a hundred wedding chapels. Besides…it's the only story we've got."

He was right. There was no other story to tell, and Murphy was pretty adamant that the provisions of Cole's grandmother's will not become public knowledge. But until this moment, she hadn't really given any thought to how hard it was going to be to look people in the eye and tell them she was a married woman, and just whom it was she was married to.

"It's just that it's kind of unbelievable," Ginny said. "Us getting married so quickly."

"It doesn't really matter whether they believe it or not. They have no way of knowing that we're not man and wife in every sense of the word, and that's all it'll take to satisfy Murphy."

Without another word, he went through the screen door into the house, letting it slap shut behind him.

Ginny wondered if things could get any more tense between her and Cole, and it turned out the answer was yes. He took her to her house, where she picked up her car and grabbed a few things to wear to work in the coming week. She decided she'd get the rest of her personal belongings later, then have an estate sale in the next few weeks to get rid of her mother's stuff, which she wasn't going to keep. The whole time they were loading things, Cole spoke to her only when it was necessary, and the rest of the time he simply acted as if she wasn't even there.

On the way from her house to the ranch, she stopped and picked up a few groceries to hold them over for a couple of days until they got settled. At the ranch, Cole helped her carry everything into the house, and she spent some time unpacking her things. She asked him which drawers he wanted and which part of the closet, but all he did was mumble something unintelligible that she took to mean, *Who cares?*

She glared at him behind his back, then took the top drawers and the part of the closet nearest the door since it was easier to get to. If he refused to make even the most basic decisions about the space they were going to occupy together for the next six months, then he would get stuck with second best. He didn't have much with him right now, anyway. He told her he'd moved all his belongings to storage in Dallas before he came to Coldwater, and all he had with him was what was in the suitcase he'd taken to Vegas, which he didn't even bother to unpack.

By the time they ate a couple of frozen spaghetti dinners, it was nearly eight o'clock. Ginny had a choice. She could spend more time with Cole at his most unfriendly or she could go to bed early. Under those circumstances, going to bed sounded wonderful.

Since he'd offered to sleep on the sofa, she brought him an extra pillow, sheets and a blanket she'd found in the closet.

He mumbled something that might have been thanks, then flipped on the television and proceeded to ignore her.

She went into the bedroom. When she finally lay down to sleep, she found herself thinking about the mixed feelings she'd had when they got to the city limits of Coldwater this afternoon. Somehow it didn't feel like home anymore. The events of the past few days had muddled her mind so much that she wasn't quite sure where she belonged, and the disorientation she felt in this unfamiliar house only added to that feeling. She was in that flux state between throwing away her old life and starting a new one, only it was going to be six months' worth of flux, living with a man she barely knew in a house so small she swore she could hear him breathe. In essence, she was trading six months of her life for twenty-five thousand dollars.

Was it worth it?

Yes. It was. She'd do anything to get out of this town. Anything to go to college, start a new life and forget this place ever existed.

Anything.

THE NEXT MORNING Ginny awoke when her alarm went off at eight o'clock. She got out of bed and shuffled into the hall, then peeked into the living room. The sheets and the blanket were folded up on the end of the sofa with the pillow on top of them. Cole was gone. Evidently he'd gone down to the barn early, as Murphy had ordered.

Later, as she drove to work, her nerves were on edge. She wished she had another day to absorb everything that had happened this weekend. She'd thought about calling in sick, but she'd never been a very good liar. Sooner or later she'd have to face the world as a married woman.

When she got to the bank, Rhonda Davenport was already there, working at the window next to Ginny as she always did. At thirty years old, Rhonda carried around about twenty extra pounds she was always trying to get rid of, but that didn't stop her from wearing too-tight pants and shirts that were a bit provocative for a woman her age. Still, Rhonda had a big heart and a ready smile for everybody. She always asked Ginny why somebody nice like her didn't have a boyfriend, which meant she was one of those people who had the ability to ignore the obvious even when it was staring her right in her face, particularly when it made somebody else feel good. Ginny thought that was a pretty nice quality to have.

On the other hand, most of the employees talked to her only within the context of her job and otherwise acted as if she didn't exist. In a way, she didn't blame them. During the six years she'd worked there, she hadn't been the most outgoing person in the world, so when it came to chatting at lunch or swapping stories or talking about what was on TV the night before, people naturally gravitated in other directions.

"Hey, Virginia!" Rhonda said, bustling around, preparing her window for the day. "I had a crummy weekend. Wanna hear about it?"

Before Ginny could say yes, no or maybe, Rhonda launched into a tirade about how her hardheaded husband, Earl, had spent four hours trying to fix the bathroom plumbing before finally flooding half the house and having to call a plumber, anyway. She talked about Earl sometimes as if he were the devil himself, but Ginny knew better. There were no two people on earth more perfect for each other than Earl and Rhonda Davenport.

"So," Rhonda said, when she finally caught a breath. "Did you have a nice weekend?"

Ginny knew it was merely a passing inquiry, like "How's it going?" or "What's new?" But sooner or later she was going to have to tell the people she worked with what had happened in the past two days, and she figured now was as good a time as any.

"Yes," she told Rhonda, who was poised to smack a roll of quarters open on her cash drawer. "My weekend was very nice. I got married."

Rhonda froze, the roll of quarters hovering in midair. She slowly set it on the counter and faced Ginny. "Come again?"

"I—I said I got married over the weekend."

Rhonda blinked dumbly, her brow furrowed with confusion. "You said married, right? As in...*married?*"

"Yes."

A grin made its way across Rhonda's mouth, and before long her whole face exploded with delight. "Well, here I was telling you all this time you oughta get yourself a boyfriend. Didn't know you'd go whole hog and head down the aisle!"

She gave Ginny a bear hug, then patted her on the cheek. "So tell me. Who's the lucky—"

"Head down the aisle?"

Ginny turned to see Susan Barker, the branch manager's assistant, and a warning bell went off in her head. Susan spent most of her time with her nose in the air, thinking she was just a little bit better than everyone else in the vicinity and most certainly better than Ginny. As usual, her blond Barbie-doll bouffant was glued in place with half a can of hairspray. Her skirt was about a foot too short to be conservative, even if she traded the hot-pink color for gray or navy.

"Virginia got married over the weekend!" Rhonda said, gushing. "Isn't that just the most exciting thing in the world?"

"Married?" Susan's mascara-laden eyes fluttered with disbelief. "I didn't even know she was engaged."

Then her gaze dropped to Ginny's left hand. Ginny immediately swept her other hand over it. "I—I haven't got a ring yet. We, uh, we only met on Friday night." She tried to laugh offhandedly, but it came out sounding weak and nervous. "It was just one of those whirlwind romances. We flew to Las Vegas, and—"

"Las Vegas? You? *You* flew to Las Vegas?"

"Yes. It was very exciting."

That was the truth. The flying part had been exciting. The getting married part—that had been excruciating.

"And romantic," Ginny added.

Okay, so that was a stretch. But wouldn't it seem a little fishy if her wedding hadn't been?

"Hey, Ruby!" Susan called. "Get out here! You're not going to believe this!"

Ruby Wallace stuck her head out of her office. She was the branch manager, a no-nonsense woman who, unlike Susan, wore colors that ranged from brown to taupe to beige to tan, with an occasional sepia thrown in. And she hadn't cracked a smile since...well, ever.

"What?" Ruby asked.

"Virginia got married over the weekend."

Ruby edged out of her office, a single dark eyebrow raised in disbelief. "Married, huh? Well. Be sure to think about whether you want to change your withholding or your insurance beneficiaries. And I'd highly recommend you take a look at your current 401-K contribution. How long have you known this man?"

"Uh, not long."

"Then steer away from joint checking. And keep whatever savings accounts you have to yourself."

"Gosh, Ruby," Rhonda said. "You're such a romantic."

"Can't be too careful," Ruby said. Ruby had been through two divorces and was working on her third. Ginny figured she probably knew what she was talking about.

In the next few seconds, the small group by Ginny's window grew larger. Bob, the security guard, and even Martha, the cleaning lady, had stopped to listen. Excitement was hard to come by around here, and everybody wanted a piece of the action. Ginny didn't like being the action they wanted a piece of.

"Well," she said, turning her gaze to her cash drawer. "Time to get to work. It's almost nine o'clock."

"Wait a minute," Susan said. "You didn't tell us his name."

"His name?"

"Yes, Virginia. You know. The man you married?"

Ginny's heart was beating ninety to nothing. She scanned the expectant faces in front of her, every one of them gawking at her as if she were their favorite soap opera star and a thrilling turning point was only seconds away. She smiled, going for that lighthearted newlywed look, knowing all the while she was failing miserably.

"His name," she said, "is Cole McCallum."

7

FOR THE COUNT of three, it was as if every molecule in the bank lobby ceased to move. Mouths hung open all over the place, and nobody seemed inclined to shut them anytime soon.

"Cole McCallum?" Susan repeated very slowly, as if she hadn't quite caught the meaning of the words. "I heard he was back in town, but...*Cole McCallum?*"

"Yes," Ginny said, trying to sound laid-back. "That's right. We met on Friday night at...at the Lone Wolf Saloon—"

"You went to the Lone Wolf?"

"Yes. I'd never been there before, but you know, it's a very fun place, and I had a few beers, and then—"

"Beers?" Susan said. "You?"

"Of course," she said quickly. "Right out of the bottle."

Susan looked at Ruby with an expression of total incredulity.

"You see," Ginny explained, "Cole remembered me from high school, and we danced, and then..."

"And then you flew to Vegas," Susan said. "You and Cole."

"No. I mean, yes, we flew to Vegas, but not until the next afternoon. We got there Saturday evening and were married that night. It was a very nice little wedding chapel, and—"

Wait. No sense lying when she'd told the truth up to now. Cupid's Little Chapel of Love had been a nuptial nightmare.

"Well, it wasn't that nice, really," she amended. "But it *was* short notice."

Dead silence. She desperately wanted somebody to say something.

Or did she?

"That's, uh, wonderful, Virginia," Susan said finally, giving the rest of the people in the vicinity a funny little smile. "Isn't it, everybody?"

Everybody nodded in conjunction with a soft chorus of assent. Then more silence. And more staring. And more of Ginny wishing she were anywhere else.

"Well, good for you!" Rhonda said finally, her cheerful voice booming through the silence. "Like I've been telling you for years now—it's time you found yourself a man."

"And a man like Cole McCallum, no less," Susan said, with a sweet little smile that didn't seem to match the expression on the rest of her face.

"Yeah," Ruby said, her gaze flicking furtively toward Susan. "Imagine that."

The silence hung on a little longer, and Ginny thought she just might be sick. Then Ruby checked her watch.

"Okay, troops," she said with a clap of her hands. "It's nearly nine o'clock. Time to get to work."

Everybody scattered, as they always did when Ruby issued an order. Ginny usually found her management style to be a bit abrupt. Now she welcomed it.

Ruby opened the doors of the bank, and a few customers straggled in, allowing Ginny the luxury of working to keep her mind off what had just happened. Maybe with luck everybody would let her pronouncement fade away.

When a couple of hours passed and nobody had said anything to her about her recent marriage, Ginny started to relax. About eleven o'clock she put her Next Window sign up and went to the bathroom. She did her business and came down the hall, only to hear voices near the teller windows.

"She said very clearly that she got married," Susan said. "*Married.* What was there to misinterpret?"

Ginny stopped in the hall, her back to the wall. She wasn't one to eavesdrop when people were gossiping, but then again, the gossip had never been about her.

"Nothing, I guess," she heard Ruby say. "But surely she didn't really mean it."

"Didn't mean what?" Susan countered. "She said that she and Cole McCallum flew to Vegas to get married. How many different ways can you interpret that?"

"Does she have a ring?" Ruby asked.

"Not yet," Rhonda said. "She said there wasn't time. That's understandable. It was a spur of the moment thing."

Susan laughed. "A spur of the moment figment of her imagination, you mean."

Ginny felt a jolt of humiliation. *Figment of her imagination?*

"I mean, if she was going to make something up, she should have at least made it believable," Susan added. "Cole McCallum. *Really.*"

"I guess she's just living in her own little dream world," Ruby said.

"She's deluded, I'd say," Susan replied. "With that weirdo mother of hers as an influence all these years, it's no wonder."

"Now y'all stop!" Rhonda said. "Who's to say she's not telling the truth?"

"Oh, come *on*, Rhonda!" Susan said. "Virginia White married to Cole McCallum? Do you really believe that hell actually froze over?"

Ginny turned and went to the bathroom, slid inside a stall and locked it behind her, suddenly feeling hot and flushed, her throat really tight as if maybe she was going to cry.

They didn't believe her. Not one word of it.

She'd expected them to question why Cole would marry her, but she'd never expected that they flat-out wouldn't believe the wedding had actually taken place. In one painful swoop, she realized just how she must have looked to these people all these years and how crazy she must sound to them. They thought she was nothing more than a poor, reclusive little person who had given in to her delusional fantasies and had started to believe one of them.

With the exception of Rhonda, she'd never counted any of these women as friends, but at least she thought they'd always respected her. To suddenly see herself as other people saw her was just about more than she could stand.

Of course, she could prove that she and Cole really were married, but what would be the point? It was obviously so unbelievable to them that they would still look at her strangely, knowing all the while that there had to be a piece of the puzzle she wasn't laying on the table. And what was she supposed to do then? Lie? Tell them that she and Cole were madly in love?

No. Of course not. She couldn't tell them that. And Cole certainly wouldn't be telling them that, either. In fact, knowing Cole, he probably wouldn't say anything at all. He'd simply shrug it off and tell her that she shouldn't give a damn what these people thought, and that would be that.

After a few minutes, it became pretty obvious to Ginny that she couldn't stay in the bathroom for a whole six months. She walked to her teller window. When Ruby and Susan saw her coming, they quickly cleared out. Rhonda gave her a friendly but bittersweet smile that said she knew she was a little misguided but she loved her anyway, which made Ginny feel like crying all over again.

Her hands were shaking as she took the next customer's deposit, and she clenched her teeth and willed them to stop. She raised her chin a little and smiled at the customer, forcing herself to think not of what her life was like now, but what her life was going to be like six months from now.

Six months. It sounded like an eternity.

COLE HADN'T liked working on the ranch ten years ago, and he didn't like it any better now, particularly with Murphy breathing down his neck.

The moment he'd stepped into the barn, the smell of horses had instantly transported him back to his senior year of high school, when Murphy had insisted he pull his own weight around the ranch. Even though he'd hated every second of it, Cole had stoically done whatever Murphy told him to do, because anything less would have verified what the man already thought—that Cole was a worthless kid following in his father's footsteps, a kid his grandmother ought to be writing off instead of taking in.

With that kind of history, Cole hadn't been the least bit surprised to find that his first assignment today involved cleaning out horse stalls.

So Cole grabbed a shovel and went after it, silently cussing Murphy with every move he made. After a couple of hours of hard labor, he was granted a reprieve when Murphy handed him the keys to his truck and told him to go to the feed store in town for some supplies.

Cole welcomed the opportunity to get away from the ranch for an hour, especially since he knew what Murphy had waiting for him when he got back. The old man had decided that today was the day they'd ride fence, which meant hours on horseback. Cole dreaded it, but he certainly wasn't going to act as if it were any big deal. No matter how hard Murphy pushed him, he had no intention of ever letting the man see him sweat.

Twenty minutes later, Cole drove into town and headed down Main Street. He stopped and picked up the supplies

Murphy wanted. Since it was nearing lunchtime, he walked across the street from the feed store to Taffy's to pick up a burger to go. He entered the restaurant, immediately assaulted by the small-town-diner smells of black coffee, ham and eggs and chicken-fried steak.

Mary Lou Culbertson sashayed over to wait on him at the counter. She wore a strangely satisfied expression that made Cole wonder what was going on.

"Hey, Cole. Funny you should show up right now. Have you heard the news?"

"News?"

The other waitresses giggled and moved in closer, ignoring their customers. Cole furtively shifted his eyes to each of them, wondering what was up. Then Mary Lou leaned her forearms on the counter, her eyebrows wiggling as if she currently possessed the juiciest piece of gossip this town had ever seen.

"Do you remember a girl named Virginia White who went to Coldwater High?" she said. "Kind of a dowdy little thing? Brown hair? Nondescript? Her mother was really weird?"

Cole eyed Mary Lou carefully. Where was she going with this? "Yeah. I remember her."

"Well, you are simply *not* going to believe this. She's running around this morning telling people—now get this—that you two are *married*."

Cole stared at Mary Lou, forcing his face to remain impassive. Why was she talking to him as if he hadn't heard about his own wedding?

Mary Lou laughed. "Isn't that the craziest thing you ever heard? I mean, that mother of hers was loony, but I never thought Virginia was insane, too. Can you imagine her making something like that up?"

Making it up? Is that what everybody thought? That Ginny had made up the fact that they were married?

erything, including what these people thought about her, and he'd come here to put an end to the gossip.

The most unexpected feeling of warmth swept through her. It wasn't just a sexual thing, even though he'd kissed her with all the intensity of a man who couldn't bear to be separated from his new wife. It was something more. She felt a bond with him she'd never felt with another person, as if they shared a secret the rest of the world would never know.

Out of the corner of her eye, she saw Susan standing to one side with a look of pure astonishment on her face.

That's right, Susan. You heard him say it. Me and Cole. Tonight. Just the two of us. And you know what newlyweds like us do when we're alone together. Why don't you sit back down at your desk and mull that one over for a while?

Just then, Ruby cleared her throat and assumed her best branch-manager voice. "You're not supposed to be back there," she told Cole. "Employees only."

"Hmm," Cole said to Ginny. "It appears that a man kissing his wife behind this counter is a breach of regulation."

Ruby cleared her throat again. Loudly.

"Can't wait for tonight," Cole said.

"Yes," Ginny said, assuming a dreamy, love-struck voice that wrapped effortlessly around her words. "Tonight."

Cole backed away from her slowly, then circled the counter and headed for the door. Everyone stood frozen in place, looking utterly flabbergasted. With one last smile in Ginny's direction, he swept out the door and closed it behind him, leaving the bank lobby in total silence.

In unison, every set of eyes turned toward Ginny. She smiled sweetly, then returned to her work as if what had just happened was no big deal at all. But beneath her calm, cool exterior, an undercurrent of excitement swept through her, a feeling of vindication that made her heart soar.

Rhonda edged next to her, a look of total disbelief on her

face. "Lordy! I don't believe I've ever seen so many stars in one man's eyes in my entire life!"

Ginny felt like hugging herself and grinning uncontrollably, but she managed to hold on to her casual attitude. "Yes," she said offhandedly. "Cole is very affectionate."

"Affectionate? That's putting it mildly. If he kisses you like that in public, I can only imagine what he does in—" Rhonda stopped herself with a flustered smile. "Sorry, sweetie, that is *none* of my business." Her gaze shifted furtively to Susan's desk, and she dropped her voice to a whisper. "I'm just so *glad* he dropped by!"

Susan was shuffling through a pile of papers, trying really hard to act as if nothing out of the ordinary had just happened. And the more she shuffled, the more obvious it was that she was on the verge of shredding, instead.

For the remainder of the day, Ginny heard the buzz of gossip all over the bank—speculation, she knew, on just where along the way Cole McCallum had lost his mind. She didn't care. She was the one who was going home to him tonight. She smiled to herself. Let them picture *that*.

Then guilt set in. She was being vindictive, on top of the fact that she was living a lie. Liars, according to her mother, were essentially thunderbolt magnets, and Ginny had to resist the urge to wonder when the next one might go whizzing past her ear. Then she thought about that big smile Cole had given her when he walked into the bank, and how it had made everybody's jaw drop to the floor, and she felt wonderful all over again.

She didn't understand anything about Cole. Nothing. One day he was negotiating a business deal with her. The next day he was angry because she wouldn't have sex with him, even though their marriage was supposed to be strictly business. Then the next day he seemed to have forgotten all about that and was acting like her loving husband to save her from malicious gossip. She just didn't understand him. Maybe it was because she didn't understand men, period.

Or maybe it was because there was a lot more to Cole McCallum than met the eye.

8

COLE HAD forgotten just how excruciating it could be to ride a horse when he hadn't been on one in years. By two o'clock his muscles were aching, and by four o'clock they were screaming in agony. He must have gotten up and down off that horse at least a hundred times during the day, using muscles he hadn't used in years, bending over, pulling wire tight, hammering in tacks to repair broken fence. He and Murphy surveyed nearly the entire perimeter of the ranch, and it was almost six o'clock before the two of them and Cliff Danbury, one of the ranch hands, finally arrived back at the barn. Cole couldn't remember the last time he'd been as exhausted or hurt as bad as he did right now.

He dismounted and led the sorrel gelding into the barn. As he took the horse's saddle off, he turned to see Cliff hauling his own saddle to the tack room. Cliff had worked on the ranch less than a month. He was a congenial kid in his early twenties, and Cole gathered that he was the type to stay around one place just long enough to save up a little cash before he was on the road again.

"Long day, huh?" Cliff stretched his arms over his head stiffly, then lowered them with a weary sigh. "Me and a couple of the other boys are heading over to the Lone Wolf for a couple of beers tonight. Wanna come along?"

The Lone Wolf. Cole never wanted to see the inside of that place again. In fact, all he could think about right now was getting a hot shower and falling into bed.

"No, thanks," Cole said. "I think I'll head to the house."

Cliff shook his head sadly. "That's what marriage'll do to you. One day you're living it up, and the next day you've got a ring through your nose and some woman leading you around. It's downright pitiful."

Cole had to agree, but he didn't figure this was the time to express those feelings when he was supposed to be a happily married man.

"I don't know, Cliff. You're going to spend half your paycheck tonight, buying drinks for women, trying to get one of them to go home with you, when I've already got one at home waiting for me." He smiled. "Which one of us is the pitiful one?"

Cliff shook his head. "You can talk it up all you want to, but I'm not buying. Who needs all that responsibility? Not to mention having sex with the same woman every night for the rest of my life." He shuddered. "No offense to your lovely wife, but I just couldn't do it."

Cole had to second that motion. The very thought of limiting himself to just one woman for the rest of his life was inconceivable to him, too. Of course, *no* women for the next six months didn't sound so hot, either.

After taking care of his horse, Cole walked the gravel road toward the foreman's house, dreaming of a hot shower and a soft bed. He saw Ginny's car out front. The moment he stepped onto the porch, he smelled something cooking.

When he opened the door, he saw Ginny at the stove, wearing a red flowered apron that hung almost to her knees. She'd pulled her hair away from her face, but a couple of strands had come loose to tumble down her cheeks. She turned when she heard the door open and smiled at him briefly. She turned away just as quickly, though, and her reluctance to meet his eyes told him she probably wasn't going to mention what had happened at the bank today. That was good. At least she wouldn't be coming down on him for breaking her no-touching rule. After all, he'd had to call a halt to the gossip, and hadn't that been the most effective way to do it?

"You're making dinner," he said. "I sure hope that's for both of us."

"Yes. It is."

Cole couldn't remember the last time he'd had any kind of meal that didn't come in a microwavable cardboard tray or a plastic box, and his mouth watered at the very thought of it.

"Good," he said. "Because I can't cook to save my life. Not that I expect you to all the time, but—"

"I don't mind. I like to cook. And since you're paying for everything for the next six months, it's only fair."

She stirred something briskly in one of the pans on the stove, a concentrated look on her face. She was such a tiny little thing that a good strong wind could have blown her away, but she bustled around like a bee around a hive. It appeared that a kitchen was one of the places she actually felt comfortable. He had a quick flashback to what he'd told Cliff about how great it was to have a woman to come home to, and for a split second it felt like the truth.

Expelling a weary breath, he hobbled to the kitchen table.

"Cole? Are you all right?"

He sank into a chair. "I'm fine."

She took a few tentative steps toward him. "You don't look fine. What happened?"

He pulled his boots off, grimacing at the effort. "Murphy picked today to ride most of the perimeter of the ranch checking the fence. Nothing like riding a horse for six hours when I haven't been on one in over ten years."

"Why today?"

"I think he wanted to remind me how much fun I had working on the ranch when I was a teenager."

"He did it on purpose?"

"Oh, you bet he did."

"Even when he saw you were hurting?"

"Especially when he saw I was hurting." He rose. "I need to get a shower."

"Okay. Dinner will be ready by the time you get out."

He walked stiffly into the bathroom, stripped off his dirty clothes and took a shower. A few minutes later, as he was drying off, he could hear Ginny rattling around in the kitchen as she finished dinner. Dinner she was cooking for both of them. Such a small thing, really, but he couldn't remember the last time anybody did anything for him.

Except maybe his grandmother.

He remembered coming home from school and she'd be there, always with a big smile and a plate of cookies or brownies. And then she'd talk to him. It had seemed so strange at first, having somebody ask him how his day had gone and then telling him all about hers. He'd rarely said much, but she'd filled in the blanks, talking when he wouldn't. Even though he'd never actually told her, those had been some of the best times of his life. It had been his first taste of how much one person could care about another person just because they shared the same blood.

Or maybe just because that person needed it badly.

God, how he missed her. He hadn't been back to see her nearly enough in the years before her death, but he'd carried her memory with him always, because it had been his one and only encounter with the notion of family. He'd always thought there was time—time to tell her that she'd meant everything to him at a point when he had nothing in his life but a mother he didn't even know and a worthless father who couldn't stay out of prison. But he'd never quite found the words. And then she'd died. A sudden stroke, and she was gone before he could even make the trip from Dallas to Coldwater.

And then he really was alone.

He got dressed and went to the kitchen. He still hurt like hell from the top of his head to the bottom of his feet, but the hot shower had taken the edge off the pain.

He pulled out a chair at the table. Ginny spun around. "You look better."

"I feel better. Need some help?"

"No. Of course not. You can barely walk. Sit down."

She didn't have to tell him twice. It felt so good to collapse in a chair and relax.

"I'll switch with you this week and I'll sleep on the sofa," she said. "At least until you're feeling better."

"You don't know what you're offering. It's not the most comfortable sofa in the world."

"I don't mind."

She pulled a casserole out of the oven and placed it on the stove top next to a bowl of green beans and a plate of hot rolls. She filled two plates and brought them to the table. After one bite, Cole knew that if this was the kind of cooking he had to look forward to for the next six months, at least his stomach was going to be happy.

"Tell me about your job at the bank," he said as they ate.

She shrugged. "It's just a job."

"You're a teller, right?"

"Uh-huh."

"What do you want to study in college? Something to do with finance?"

"Maybe." She shrugged, staring at her food. "I'll be filling out the application soon. My grades were good in high school. I don't think I'll have any problem being accepted."

"That's good."

She focused on her chicken casserole, teasing her fork through it. "Yes. Probably finance. I imagine there are a lot of job possibilities with that major."

"Why don't you look at me when you talk?"

She jerked her head up. "What?"

"You don't look people in the eye very often. Are you afraid to?"

"Afraid?"

"Have something to hide?"

"No!"

"Am I that ugly?"

Her eyes flew open wide. "Of course not!"

"There. That's better."

She looked at her plate again. He caught her chin with his fingertips and eased her head up. "I don't know why you act like a scared rabbit most of the time, but I wish you'd stop it. I don't want to spend the next six months talking to the top of your head."

He didn't know why, but he let his hand linger in just that position, with his fingertips beneath her chin, looking into her eyes. For the first time he noticed that there were flecks of gold spattered against the dark brown of her irises.

Beautiful.

That was the word that came to mind, though he knew it couldn't possibly be true. Ginny was as plain as any woman he'd ever known. So why was it when he looked into her eyes right now, he suddenly saw so much more?

Finally he let his fingertips fall from her face. To his surprise she didn't turn away. Her gaze softened, and a warm light entered her eyes.

"Thank you," she said. "For what you did today."

Suddenly he was the one who had the urge to look away. "It was just a little kiss, Ginny. No big deal."

"You know it was more than that. You didn't have to...to go to those lengths. I just want you to know I appreciate it."

She continued to stare at him, and it made him feel very uneasy. "Actually," he told her, "I'm surprised you're not mad at me for breaking the rule."

"The rule?"

"No touching."

She turned away instantly, and he responded by leaning closer to her. "Of course, if you'd like me to break the rule a few more times, I'm sure I can arrange it."

She spun around. "What?"

"And while you're at it," he added, "feel free to make a few more rules, and we'll break those, too."

She looked at him with disbelief. "Cole, just because you kissed me at the bank, it doesn't mean—"

"Are you sure, Ginny?" he said, running his fingertips along her arm. "I think you were enjoying yourself when I kissed you. Wouldn't you like to enjoy yourself a little more?"

Slowly she narrowed her eyes into a sharp, angry glare, then yanked her arm away from him and stood up. She grabbed their empty dinner plates, took them to the sink and dropped them with a clatter. She twisted the faucet, splashing water on the plates, then turned it off just as abruptly. Cole stared at her with astonishment.

"Come on, Ginny! What are you getting so mad about?"

She dried her hands on a dish towel, then flung it to the counter and headed toward the hall. She stopped at the doorway and spun around.

"It was a nice thing you did today, Cole. Maybe the nicest thing anybody's ever done for me. So why do you have to be such a jerk when all I was trying to do was say thank-you?"

Jerk?

He rose from his chair and circled the table. "Hey! All I did was suggest that it might be nice to pick up where we left off today. Would that really be so awful?"

"But we've been through all this before!"

He stopped in front of her. "You can protest all you want to. But the truth is that you want it as much as I do. And if you don't give in sooner or later, it's going to be a very long six months for both of us."

"I have no intention of giving in to anything!"

Cole threw up his hands in frustration. "God, Ginny, do you have to be so uptight? Sex is good. Sex is fun. Sex is—"

"No!"

She turned to head down the hall, but he caught her arm and turned her around. "Hold on, now," he said gently, knowing he was on the verge of making yet another tactical error. "Just listen to me for a minute, will you?"

He lowered his voice, softening it around the edges, which was a tough thing to do considering his current frustration level. But he reminded himself of just how ineffective a strong come-on had been in Vegas, and he had no desire to repeat that experience. He had to remember how young and innocent she really was.

"Now, sweetheart," he began, "I know you may not understand this because you've never had a relationship before, but men...well, men are a little different from women. They have certain...needs."

She swallowed hard but met his gaze evenly. "If that's true, then I suppose you'll be wanting to go somewhere else to fulfill those needs."

Cole blinked. "What?"

"I can't stop you, Cole. But if you decide to be with another woman, please do me a favor and be discreet."

He stood there, stunned. He'd assumed it was just a fragile wall that separated them, one he could knock down with a flick of his fingers. Instead it was an impenetrable fortress he wasn't even going to be able to blast his way through. This was not just a matter of getting her to loosen up a little. She truly didn't want him. She was legally and morally free to have him, and still she didn't want him. And she was making it quite clear that she never would.

The blow to his pride was greater than he ever would have imagined. This little waif of a woman who should have been so easy to seduce was turning him away. For the next six months, he was going to be sharing a house with a woman he couldn't lay a finger on.

Then he told himself it didn't matter, that he should be keeping his eyes on the prize. In six months, when he sold this ranch and got back on top again, women would be standing in line to jump into his bed. Beautiful women. Stunning women.

Willing women.

Then again, six months was a long time. He was a man who was used to making things happen quickly, so it sounded like forever. Could he really wait that long?

Did he *have* to wait that long?

"You know what, sweetheart?" he said. "That's not such a bad idea. Thanks for the suggestion. And of course I'll be discreet," he added, with a touch of sarcasm. "I've got a twelve-hundred-acre ranch riding on it."

He strode into the kitchen, yanked on his boots, grabbed his car keys and stormed out of the house.

WHAT A HELL of a way to spend an evening.

Cole had stalked out of the house with every intention of grabbing the first woman he came into contact with and satisfying that need he'd talked so big about, but by the time he reached the city limits of Coldwater, his foot wasn't quite so heavy on the gas pedal, and his enthusiasm was starting to wane at the prospect of woman hunting. He drove through town, then turned onto the state highway and kept moving down the road, and before he knew it, he'd reached the city limits of Tyler.

Damn. What was he going to do now?

He could go home.

No. Then he'd be admitting to Ginny that he'd rather be home having her turn a cold shoulder to him than be out on the town living it up.

He spotted a movie theater and pulled into the parking lot. He went into the lobby, where he bought a ticket to the next movie playing. A couple of fairly attractive women were giving him suggestive looks, and with Tyler being a reasonably large town, he could have slipped away for a few hours with one of them and nobody would have been the wiser.

Nobody but him.

What was the matter with him, anyway? He wasn't married to Ginny. Not really. So why was he acting like a man who was thinking of cheating on his wife?

Because she looked at you like that. Like you were betraying her.

He sat through the movie—some dumb action-adventure thing with lots of cussing and gunfire and explosions—but he found the more he tried to concentrate on it, the more he thought about Ginny. He thought about what had happened at the bank today. And he thought about her thanking him for it. And by the time the movie was over and the credits were rolling, he was thinking, *She's right. You really are a jerk.*

When he'd gone over to that bank this morning, he'd told himself that his intent was to settle an old score with the people of Coldwater, to make them eat some of their hateful gossip for a switch, but that was only part of it. Mostly he'd gone over there because he didn't want to leave Ginny out in the cold to bear the brunt of it all by herself. Yet when she thanked him for it, what had he done?

He'd acted like a jerk.

It was after ten o'clock by the time he pulled onto the ranch and drove down the road to the foreman's house. It was dark, which, thankfully, meant Ginny was asleep, so he wouldn't have to face her tonight. He got out of his car and came through the kitchen door. As he shut it behind him, he heard a voice in the darkness.

"Cole?"

He flinched at the sudden sound, then flipped on the kitchen light and glanced into the living room.

"Ginny? Why aren't you in bed?"

She rose up on one elbow. "I told you I'd sleep on the sofa."

If he hadn't already felt like the jerk she'd said he was, he certainly did now. He'd stormed out of here like some kind of an idiot, threatening to go find a woman who would put out because Ginny wouldn't, and here she was sleeping on that bag of bricks because she didn't want him to be uncomfortable.

She sat up, her hair sleep-mussed, and he saw she was wearing one of those all-encompassing nightgowns she seemed so fond of. He came into the living room, but as he drew closer, she leaned away, pulling the blanket over her breasts.

Cole sighed with frustration. Never in his life had a woman reacted to him like this. Never. Then again, would she be so shy around him if only he'd kept his promise and kept his distance?

He sat down on the end of the sofa, resting his elbows on his knees, his hands clasped together. "Do you know where I was tonight?"

"No," she said quickly. "And I don't want to know."

"I went to a movie. I left here, drove to Tyler, saw a movie and came home."

The silence was so complete he could hear the kitchen clock ticking. Glancing sideways, he saw that her eyes had grown wide and disbelieving, her face peeking over that blanket she'd pulled almost up to her chin.

"Was it...a good movie?"

"Yeah," he said. "Wonderful."

"Why didn't you...?"

"Why didn't I do what I said I was going to do? Hell, Ginny, I don't know." He stared at his hands, tapping his fingertips together, then turned to look at her. "Why did you suggest it in the first place?"

She shrugged. "You said you had...needs."

He squeezed his eyes closed. "Do you think we can forget I ever said that?"

"Forget it?"

"Yeah. And maybe even forget about the rest of tonight, too. The part after dinner, anyway."

She stared at him with a confused expression. He didn't blame her.

"I suppose we could."

He nodded. "Good. That's good."

They sat in silence for a long time. Cole tried to think of something else to say that might make this situation feel a little less awkward, but nothing came to him. Finally he stood up.

"I'm going to bed."

She nodded.

He started toward the bedroom. Then he stopped and turned back, thinking it was time he righted another wrong.

"Just for the record," he said, "I think it's downright ridiculous for either of us to have to sleep on that nightmare of a sofa when we can share a halfway comfortable bed."

"Cole—"

He held up his palm. "It's not what you think. I swear I won't touch you, Ginny. I know now that you're serious about that, and I'll keep my promise."

Her eyes widened with that look of wariness he was coming to know so well—the one he really wished he could make disappear.

"See, I'm kind of hoping that when I go into that bedroom right now, you'll come with me, but if you don't believe I'll keep my word, it's okay. You can stay out here."

Ginny huddled under the blanket, wanting desperately to trust him. She couldn't believe he'd gone to a movie. Cole McCallum, who collected women like other people collected coins or stamps, went to a *movie*.

The question was, why? When she'd practically given him an engraved invitation to go find another woman, he'd chosen not to.

Still, no matter how sincere he sounded, she couldn't make herself get up from the sofa. Seconds ticked by. Finally he sighed with resignation.

"Good night, Ginny."

She watched Cole disappear into the hall, his boots clunking against the hardwood floor. Once he was gone, the silence seemed to scream at her, echoing the frustration she felt.

Just when she thought maybe she had Cole figured out, he did something that shook everything up all over again. He seemed so impossibly complicated she didn't think she'd ever understand him. One thing she did know, though, was that when he'd asked her to join him in bed and she'd refused, he'd actually looked disappointed. Not disappointed that she wasn't going to be sharing his bed in a husband-wife sense, but disappointed that he'd offered her something in friendship and she'd turned it down.

Ginny pushed the blanket away and stood up. She walked to the bedroom door. It was ajar. Peering inside, she saw Cole was already in bed.

She pushed the door open and walked into the room. By the light of the moon streaming through the window, she saw he had the blankets pulled up only to his waist, leaving his chest bare. Just the sight of it made her mouth go dry, and she wondered what he had on, or *didn't* have on, beneath those blankets.

Just as she was thinking maybe this was a bad idea, he shifted and pulled the sheets aside for her to lie down next to him. Crazy warning thoughts rushed through her mind. *What if this really is just a ploy to get me into his bed? What if he really does want sex?*

What if I decide I want it, too?

It was that third one that really got to her, because when it came right down to it, Cole wasn't the only one she wondered if she could trust. She'd thought more about sex in the past three days than she ever had in her life, and she didn't know if she was up to telling him no one more time.

She took a deep breath and lay down, resting her head on the pillow, and he pulled the covers gently over her. As he pulled his arm away, it brushed against her breast, and a raw, hot sensation streaked through her body. For a moment, she thought she'd made a terrible mistake. Then Cole shifted over and lay beside her. He let out a long, relaxing breath, and then he was still.

A minute passed, maybe two. Then she heard his voice in the darkness.

"Say it again."

She turned just enough that she could see the silhouette of his face in the moonlight. "What?"

"What you said to me at dinner tonight. About what happened at the bank."

It took a moment for her to understand. "I appreciate what you did for me today," she said softly. "Thank you."

"You're welcome. Good night, Ginny."

She smiled to herself. "Good night, Cole."

After a few minutes the soft cadence of his breathing told her he'd fallen asleep. But Ginny was nowhere near sleep. Instead she lay wide awake, so aware of the man sleeping beside her that she swore she could feel every beat of his heart.

She slid her hand over her own heart. It was hammering in her chest like crazy. Is this how she was going to feel every night she went to bed with Cole? As if her heart were going to beat right out of her chest?

If so, the months ahead were going to feel like years.

9

"HEY, GINNY!" Rhonda said. "How's that new husband of yours doing?"

Ginny stuffed a stack of twenties into her cash drawer with a silent sigh. Rhonda asked her that just about every day, and Ginny always answered with some bright little affirmative that made Rhonda smile real big and say something like, "Glad the honeymoon is still going strong," or "It must be nice to sit out under the stars with your husband on that great big ranch," or just, "I'm so glad you're happy, sweetie—it's about time." But after several weeks, as much as she loved Rhonda, her comments were starting to wear on Ginny's nerves.

"He's doing okay," Ginny said. "Staying busy on the ranch."

"Keeping you busy, too, I'll bet." Rhonda winked, and Ginny smiled in return, when in reality she wanted to scream.

It wasn't as if Cole was hard to live with. By the time July passed and August came, they'd settled into a comfortable routine. He appreciated her cooking and said so all the time. He respected her privacy as much as one person could, given the size of the space they were occupying, no matter what he'd said about how impossible it was going to be. And it was nice to sit around in the evening with him watching television, because it turned out both of them loved historical documentaries and sitcoms and hated reality TV and obnoxious talk shows.

Since they'd moved in, Cole had fixed the bathroom plumbing and patched the leaking roof to keep the place livable, while Ginny had planted pink petunias along the front porch and hung a wreath on the door to try to make it at least a little more homey.

And whenever they left the ranch to go into town, Cole was very attentive to her, playing the part of a newlywed husband and doing so convincingly. Even when they got the strangest stares from the townspeople, Cole pretended he didn't see a thing, and not long after, she found herself doing the same. And soon, to her surprise, people stopped staring. Ginny was sure they were still talking behind their backs, but they *did* stop staring.

The days were okay. It was the nights that were driving her crazy.

Every night when Cole shut off the lamp and lay on his pillow beside her, Ginny's heart did a little flip-flop. Even though he'd kept his promise and things had stayed platonic between them, she found herself thinking constantly about the way he'd kissed her and what it might be like if he did it again. And just as quickly as the thought would cross her mind, she'd try to chase it away, because after all this time, she still couldn't get her mother's loud, condemning voice out of her mind.

Every shift of Cole's body on the mattress would spur one fantasy or another, and a little twinge of guilt would race through her. Then she'd get angry at herself for feeling guilty. Then she'd get angry at her mother for making her feel that way. And then she'd chastise herself for her anger, and the guilt would set in all over again.

"Cole?" she said one night after the lights were out.

He stirred, then turned to look at her. "Yes?"

"Do you think it's possible to love somebody and hate them all at the same time?"

The moment the words were out of her mouth, she wanted to yank them back. What would Cole—what would *anybody*—think of such a question? But then she heard his voice, calm and even, without a hint of a judgmental tone.

"I don't know. Who did you have in mind?"

She paused a long time, then whispered, "My mother."

There was a silence. He probably thought she was crazy. Maybe she *was* crazy.

Cole shifted to face her. "I'm not really all that tired. Why don't you tell me about her?"

Ginny had never said a derogatory word to anyone about her mother—ever—so right now she felt as if she were on the verge of committing a mortal sin.

"She was my mother, and I loved her, but..." She exhaled, closing her eyes, not really sure how to put it into words.

"Tell me what she was like," Cole said.

"Intense," Ginny said, staring at the ceiling, "and very dictatorial. She quoted the Bible a lot, even though we never went to church. She thought most everything was a sin."

She glanced at Cole. He simply stared at her, waiting for her to continue.

"When I was growing up, she found fault with any friend I ever had. The few times I got up the nerve to invite other kids over, she treated them so rudely that they never came back. Pretty soon I quit trying. She wouldn't let me dress like the other girls, or wear makeup, or even cut my hair."

"So the other kids made fun of you?"

"Most of the time it didn't even go that far. At least then they would have been acknowledging me. When they looked at me, it was as if they didn't see me at all. I was just a nobody. That was fine with my mother, because she thought the whole rest of the world was sinful, and it was probably best if I didn't associate with them anyway."

"You were lonely, then."

Ginny's stomach twisted at the memory. She thought about all those endless days of being ignored and of all the time she'd spent alone in her bedroom with the same dreams as every other little girl, only she'd had absolutely no way of realizing them.

"Yes," she whispered.

"Where was your father?"

"I never knew him. My mother did—for one night. And then he disappeared. I think she resented me as much as she resented him because I reminded her every day of the mistake she'd made in trusting him."

"But later you still lived with your mother, even though you were an adult?"

"She was sick. She needed me."

"What was the matter with her?"

Ginny shrugged. "I don't know. This and that."

"So nothing in particular and everything in general."

That was it exactly. Ginny had never known for sure what was wrong with her mother because her mother never went to a doctor, but still she was in bed most of the time and wanted her daughter to wait on her hand and foot.

"How did she die?" Cole asked.

"A sudden heart attack."

"So nothing really related to her aches and pains."

"I don't think so. Not really."

"So how did you feel when she was gone?"

Ginny's throat tightened. She couldn't say it. Those few words that were jammed inside her mind just wouldn't come out, because she knew if she spoke them, something terrible was sure to befall her.

"You felt relieved," Cole said.

She stared at him in disbelief. The very words she couldn't say herself had just come out of his mouth.

"No," she said quickly. "Not relieved. Not exactly. I—"

"Ginny," he said gently. "You were twenty-four years old, and suddenly you had a life of your own. It's not your fault that it took your mother's death to finally let you experience that. And I don't think you really hated her. You just didn't know how to deal with her, and that's nothing to feel guilty about."

Ginny stared into the darkness. "But she talks to me inside my head, Cole. She's still telling me every move I make is a sin, and it's so hard to ignore it. I hear it all the time, day in and day out, until I want to scream."

"So why don't you just tell her to shut up?"

Ginny whipped around to stare at Cole. "What?"

"Tell her to shut up. God, Ginny, she's yelling at you from beyond the grave. It's not like she's going to be able to back up whatever she yells at you about."

Ginny blinked with total disbelief.

"You're a rational adult. You know now that your mother had a lot of problems. *She* had problems. You didn't. And if you keep listening to her, you'll never have a life of your own."

She stared at him, overcome with the oddest feeling. It was as if the hazy, hard-to-understand things about her mother were suddenly coming into sharp focus.

She had a lot of problems.

That was an understatement.

Keep listening to her, and you'll never have a life.

And Ginny wanted a life. Desperately.

"So the next time you pick up that phone inside your head and it's her," Cole said, "just hang up."

Ginny was astonished. *Just hang up?*

"It's as simple as that?" she asked.

"No. Not really. But it's a start."

He'd stated the truth so simply that for the first time her

guilt seemed to fade into the background and her mother's voice was almost impossible to hear.

"For the record, Ginny, you're not alone with the love-hate thing. I felt the same way about my father."

As soon as he said the words, he rolled over, his back to her, and was silent. Ginny wanted to ask a hundred questions about that, but he was clearly telling her that now wasn't the time.

Long after she knew Cole was asleep, she still lay awake. She couldn't deny the attraction she felt to him, and it was growing by the day. It had been much easier to keep him at arm's length in the beginning, but the more she got to know him, the more she was drawn to him. She was starting to see that his reputation didn't begin to indicate the kind of person he really was any more than hers did. And he understood about her mother. Really understood.

And she had the feeling there was a lot about him that needed understanding, too.

ONE SEPTEMBER EVENING a few weeks later, Ginny sat on the back porch sipping a cup of herbal tea. An unexpectedly cool breeze tossed her hair, and she wondered how long it would be before the shorter days would make the trees start to turn. Soon the ranch would come alive with blazing autumn colors, and she couldn't wait to see that.

She hadn't seen Cole yet this evening. He'd told her that he was meeting a man in town to discuss some business and he might not be home for dinner. He didn't bother to share with her the nature of his business, and she didn't ask. Still, she'd heard him talking on the phone a couple of times in the past few days, and just the bits and pieces she'd overheard told her it had something to do with a commercial real-estate project.

He was planning ahead already.

She started thinking about how much money the ranch would bring when Cole eventually sold it. Since he was willing to give her twenty-five thousand dollars, it had to be worth far, far more than that. It was twelve hundred acres, and with that beautiful ranch house and a spectacular stable, it had to be worth quite a lot of money. And according to Cole, his grandmother had raised some of the finest quarter horses in the country, and they were obviously valuable, too.

Ginny looked down the road to the barn in the distance, settling her gaze on the horses milling around in the corrals behind it. She'd resisted the urge to go see them up close because even though she was drawn to horses, she was a little scared of them, too. Cole had told her it might be okay to ride one sometime, but since he was always so tired when he came in at night she didn't want to ask him to go down there. And she certainly couldn't ride one by herself.

Maybe she could just go down there and *look* at them.

After arguing with herself for a few more minutes, she finally went into the house. She put on her jeans, thinking she ought to dress for the occasion, then walked down the gravel road to the barn. Peeking inside, she saw a double row of horse stalls with a hay-filled loft over them, and her nose was assaulted by the scent of hay and grain and the strong but not unpleasant smell of horses.

She walked to the first stall and saw a big, shiny red horse with black legs and a black mane and tail. There was a white stripe down its face, and its right hind leg was white about halfway up to its knee.

She slid her hand over the stall door and made a little clucking noise with her tongue. The horse's ears perked up, then it walked over slowly and stretched its neck out to sniff Ginny's hand. The feel of the horse's warm breath and the whiskers brushing against her palm sent tingles racing up her arm.

Then Ginny heard footsteps. She whipped around to see Murphy approaching, and immediately she yanked her hand out of the stall. She'd had very little contact with him since she'd come here, but given the way he glared at Cole anytime he saw him, he clearly wasn't going to think much of having her around, either.

"I was just petting her," Ginny said quickly. "But if you don't want me to—"

"Petting's fine," Murphy said, stopping beside her. "As long as you're out here and she's in there."

"Is she...dangerous?"

His lip quirked. "Nah. Not this one. But she's just awful big, and you're awful little. All she'd have to do is step on your toes and you'd be pretty sorry."

"She's so beautiful," Ginny said.

"She was a champion in her day. She's getting on in years now."

Ginny brushed a fly off the mare's neck. "I've always loved horses."

"You ever ride before?" Murphy asked.

"No, but I'd like to." She stole a glance at him. "Is it hard?"

"Depends on the horse."

Ginny nodded. "Would this one be hard to ride?"

"Nah. A five-year-old could ride her."

She patted the horse's nose. "What's her name?"

"Well, she's got a big old long registered name, but we just call her Sunday."

"Was she born on a Sunday?"

"Yep. One minute after midnight. Edna looked at her watch and said, 'It's Sunday,' and it kind of stuck."

Ginny smiled. "So you were there?"

"Oh, yeah. I've seen most of them born on this ranch for the past twenty years." Murphy scratched the mare's neck. "Why don't we saddle her up so you can ride?"

Ginny felt a surge of excitement. "Really? Could I?"

Murphy went into a room in the barn and brought out a saddle and bridle. After saddling the horse, he led her to the arena adjoining the barn and showed Ginny how to mount. After three tries, she finally managed to pull herself up. She swung her leg over the mare's back and plopped down in the saddle. Murphy adjusted the stirrups, then handed her the reins. He showed her how to hold them and how to do something called neck reining.

Pretty soon she was walking Sunday around the rail of the arena, her stomach fluttering with exhilaration. Murphy called out commands, telling her to keep her heels down in the stirrups and to take up some of the slack in the reins. Doing everything all at once wasn't easy, but Sunday didn't seem to mind when she pulled the reins funny or sat crooked. It was all pretty confusing at first, but after a few minutes she felt comfortable enough to take Murphy's advice and bump her heels against the horse and nudge her into a trot. She found that to be a whole lot more uncomfortable than walking, but as long as she held on to the saddle horn she didn't feel as if she was going to fall. Murphy said that pretty soon she'd learn to move with the horse instead of against her.

After she finished her first riding lesson and Murphy unsaddled the horse, he gave Ginny a brush and showed her how to use it, telling her to be careful not to brush too hard on the mare's flanks or legs. Then he handed her a comb and pointed to the mare's tail.

"Stand to one side," he told her. "Even though Sunday won't kick, some other horse might, so you'd better get used to doing it right."

"Like this?" she said.

"Yeah." Murphy took the brush and rubbed it over the mare's back. "How much did Cole offer you to play his wife for six months?"

Ginny turned, startled, her cheeks burning with embarrassment. "Uh, nothing. I—I just…"

Her voice trailed off. She wanted to lie, *tried* to lie, but Murphy's sharp, blue-eyed gaze was boring right into her.

"Twenty-five thousand dollars," she murmured.

Murphy gave a low whistle.

"See, I—I want to go to college. I've wanted to go for such a long time, but it would have taken me forever to save the money, and—"

"Well. That explains a lot. Like why a nice girl like you would give herself to a man she barely knows."

"I'm not giving myself to him. Not—not like you think."

She felt a rush of embarrassment again and returned to her tail combing, wishing Murphy hadn't brought up any of this.

"The minute he gets title to this ranch, you know he's going to sell it," Murphy said.

Ginny was silent.

"And that's the last you'll ever see of him."

"I don't care. I have my own plans."

"Time's gonna pass, though, and you may have a tendency to start thinking otherwise." Murphy's mouth was set in a taut line of disapproval. "He'll hurt you if you let him, Ginny. And he won't think twice about it."

"I don't think he's like that," she said. "Not really."

"His grandmother thought that, too. She was blind when it came to Cole, thinking he was different from his father. Do you know he only came back here four times? Four times in ten years, after everything Edna did for him. She invited him back for every holiday, even though I told her he wouldn't come. But still she hoped he would."

"Maybe there was a reason—"

"No. No reason. Just lack of gratitude. He had his grandmother snowed, and it looks like he's got you snowed, too."

"No. He's not like that. He's—"

She stopped short, unable to find the words to express to Murphy that she saw something in Cole maybe nobody had ever seen before. Nobody, maybe, except his grandmother. But even if she found the words, she knew Murphy wouldn't believe them.

"I—I think I'd better go," she said. She set the comb on the edge of the stall door and started to leave the barn. She'd just about gotten out the door when Murphy called to her.

"Sunday's yours for the time you're here, if you want her."

Ginny whirled around with a small, involuntary gasp, her hand flying to her chest. "Really?"

"I'll tell the boys not to turn her out to pasture. But that means you need to ride her every day or she won't get the exercise she needs. You can come back tomorrow night for another lesson if you want to."

"Oh! I will!"

Ginny felt a surge of excitement. This was going to be like having her very own horse.

Then Murphy's face grew serious again. "Where Cole's concerned," he said, "I just want you to keep your eyes open."

She knew there was another part to that warning he wasn't saying.

And your heart closed.

10

"It's a two-hundred-unit building, built in the twenties, all brick, minimal structural problems. It's next to a residential area that's on the upswing, and the numbers look good."

Cole sat in the back booth at Taffy's, drinking a cup of coffee and listening to Dave Fletcher try to sell him on some run-down rattrap on the outskirts of Morrison Heights, a suburb of Dallas filled with early-twentieth-century homes and apartments. Morrison Heights was nice in the areas where renovation had been done and a hellhole where it hadn't.

"What's the current occupancy?"

"Seventy percent."

"Which means the other thirty percent is rotting away."

"Yep," Fletcher said. "Which is why we can get it for fifty percent of market value. Maybe less."

He went on to spell out a few more of the numbers—owner financing, possible tax advantages, government money that might be available to assist with some of the rehab. Cole had to admit that the longer the guy talked, the better it sounded.

Then Fletcher pulled a stack of photos out of his pocket. Cole flipped through them. The complex had all brick buildings and nice architecture. Yes, the wood trim was rotting, but the basic structure was there. He started to envision exterior paint, awnings, brass fixtures, landscaping. He looked at some interior photos and saw arched doorways, crown moldings and solid-oak floors. The place was a renovator's dream, as long as he had plenty of money to play with. But it was a deal only if the rents could be at least tripled on completion of the project.

"It's not close enough to downtown," Cole said. "It may be hard to get tenants at the rents we'd have to set."

Fletcher leaned forward, folding his arms on the table in front of him. "Well, my friend, that's where the risk comes in, doesn't it? But then, you've never been one to let a little thing like that get in your way. I'm betting you can make it enough of a draw that the location won't be as big an issue."

Fletcher was a player, and a good one at that. But Cole wondered whether he might be stepping out on a limb with this one.

"So when will you be coming into that chunk of cash you told me about?" Fletcher asked.

It was the first week of September. He'd take title to the ranch in about three months. But how long would it take to sell it after that?

"Hard to say. Several months at least."

"If I bump the purchase price just a little, I think the owner will go for a one-year option. I'll put up the option money. That's a drop in the bucket. All you need to do is come through with your half of the purchase price at closing."

Fletcher wasn't talking about much money compared to what Cole would have upon the sale of the ranch, and it was just the kind of project that made his blood rush.

"You sure you want to mess with me, Fletcher? Some people think I set fires."

"You've always shot straight with me. That's all I give a damn about. Besides, you're the only guy I know who's got the vision and the guts to tackle this project."

Cole leaned back in his chair. "I'm not too hot on the idea of taking on a partner right about now. Any partner. No offense."

Fletcher smiled. "None taken. But I know you better than

that. I don't care what's happened in the past. If you smell money in a deal, you'll be all over it. And I think you've got a whiff now, don't you?"

Cole stared at him, his brain moving like lightning, putting the photos and the numbers together, and the more he thought about it, the better it seemed. He felt that rush of adrenaline, the one that always swept through him whenever a deal came together.

"Just give me a little nod here, McCallum. That's all I'm asking for right now."

Cole tapped his coffee cup with his fingertip. No risk right now, with possibly a big payoff in the future. He couldn't lose.

"Get the option," he said.

Fletcher smiled. "I knew I came to the right place." He stood up and tossed a ten on the table. "I'll be in touch."

DRIVING BACK to the ranch, Cole stepped on the gas a little heavier than usual, feeling his Porsche corner smoothly along the curves of the state highway. His heart beat faster than usual, his mind truly at work for the first time since he'd come to Coldwater.

Fletcher had been right. He smelled money in this one, and he had nothing to lose when somebody else was putting up the option money. Soon he would have the capital to put into the project and be flying high again, rising to that place where his life was his own and nobody could touch him.

He came into the kitchen to find Ginny sitting at the table, thumbing through a magazine.

She looked up with a smile. "Hi."

"Hi." He sat down at the table and pulled off his boots.

"Did you get dinner?" she asked. "I have leftovers—"

"No. It's okay. I ate at Taffy's."

He looked across the table at the magazine she was reading. *"Western Horseman?"*

"Yeah."

"Where'd you get that?"

"Murphy gave it to me."

"Murphy? Why?"

"He thought I'd like it. He's teaching me how to ride."

Cole stared at her with surprise. "You're kidding."

"No. I rode a horse named Sunday. Murphy taught me about saddling her, and then I rode some, and then he showed me how to brush her."

"Murphy did all that?"

"Yes. He was actually very nice."

Cole couldn't believe it. Were they talking about the same grouchy old man?

"Riding is so much fun," Ginny said, her face glowing. "Maybe you can come down some evening and—"

"I do plenty of riding during the day, Ginny. I don't need an evening of it, too."

He spoke a little more harshly than he intended to, but something about Murphy being so nice to Ginny really put him on his guard. What did the old man hope to accomplish by doing that? Turn her against him?

"Just remember that Murphy is liable to say some pretty nasty things about me."

Ginny smiled. "Don't worry. I don't necessarily believe everything that Murphy says about you."

"Good."

"And I don't necessarily believe everything that you say about Murphy, either."

She looked at her magazine with a self-satisfied smile, and all at once Cole realized it had been a long time since she'd cowered around him like she used to. When she spoke to him now she looked him right in the eye and didn't flinch. And the sight of her sweet little face wearing that smug expression made him wonder if that was good or bad.

She's not what you thought she was, he realized in a flash of insight. *She's one hell of a lot more.*

He watched her for several seconds as she focused on the magazine, her chin resting in her hand, her golden-brown hair falling in thick strands along her cheeks.

She looked up and saw him staring. "What?"

For the hundredth time, he thought, *She's not beautiful*. So why was it sometimes he just couldn't take his eyes off her?

"Uh...nothing."

He rose and headed to the living room, where he flipped on the television. Ginny joined him a few minutes later.

"What are you watching?" she asked.

"It's September. And this is Monday night."

"So?"

"Football. The Cowboys' season opener is tonight."

"Oh," she said with a disinterested sigh. "Football."

"Don't tell me you've never seen a football game."

"I've never seen a football game."

He recoiled, giving her a look of utter disbelief. "That's downright un-American."

She rolled her eyes.

"Tell you what, sweetheart," he said, patting the sofa cushion. "Why don't you sit right here and I'll teach you all about it."

"I don't *want* to learn all about it."

"Then you'll really be in the dark every Sunday afternoon and every Monday night, not to mention Saturdays with college ball."

"You're going to be watching all those times?"

"Yes, and that's absolutely nonnegotiable."

"Sorry. Everything's negotiable." She thought for a moment. "Let's see...for every football game we watch, you have to give me two cooking shows."

Cole screwed up his face with disgust. "Two for one? How fair is that?"

"Plenty fair when football games are hours long. Even I know that."

"Can I sleep through the cooking shows?"

"As long as you keep your hands off the remote."

He gave her a sidelong glance. "You ever think about investing in real estate? It's all in the negotiating, you know."

"I'm keeping my options open." Ginny sat on the sofa. "Speaking of real estate, how was your meeting tonight?"

Cole stared at her. "You knew what my meeting was about?"

"Your voice carries when you're on the phone."

So she knew what he was up to, and she was smart enough to know what it meant. But it didn't matter. They had a deal, and she'd known from the beginning that he intended eventually to sell the ranch and pocket the money for investment purposes.

So why did he feel so guilty?

He shrugged off that feeling, even as he sensed that she wanted to know more. She didn't ask, though. Good thing, because he didn't want to tell her. What he did with the money this ranch would bring him at sale was nobody's business but his.

GINNY HAD NO IDEA that watching a football game could be such an excruciating experience.

It had nothing to do with the game itself. As games went, football was pretty interesting. But not half as interesting as Cole.

At the start of the game, he'd taken her hand and pulled her right down next to him, her thigh only inches from his.

Normally when they watched TV they occupied separate ends of the sofa, but here they were, sitting as close as…well, as close as if they were married.

Move over, she'd told herself about a thousand times since the game started, but then Cole would lean into her and point at something on the screen, and the heat from his body would send warm shivers flowing through her. He'd casually tap her arm or her leg every once in a while to get her attention, and although he did it in the most platonic way possible, every time he touched her she practically jumped right out of her skin. Even the low, husky quality of his voice as he patiently explained first downs and field goals and penalties made her a little light-headed, until she was sure she'd never remember a single word of what he was telling her.

He was keeping his promise. He was acting as if they were just two friends watching a football game together. Nothing more. But the longer she sat only inches away from Cole, the more she realized that keeping him segregated to the friends side of her brain was a very difficult thing to do.

As halftime approached, she closed her eyes for a moment and imagined what it would be like if they were really married and were watching the game together. Would they carry on their own halftime activities and forget all about the rest of the game?

A montage of the kisses Cole had given her, at the Lone Wolf, in Vegas, in the bank, flashed in her mind, hot, sensual kisses that had put all her senses on red alert. Pretty soon she was imagining his lips on other parts of her body, as well. A hot blush rose on her cheeks, and it was all she could do not to leap up to splash icy water on her face.

Casual conversation. That's what she needed. Bland, sexless words coming out of her mouth to stop the spicy, sexy thoughts running through her mind.

"The Cowboys play in Dallas, right?" she asked. "Did you ever go to football games when you lived there?"

"Yeah. A couple of times. I even thought about getting season tickets once."

"I bet they're expensive."

"Yeah, but I could have afforded it. Back then, anyway."

"Before the fire."

The words slipped out before she really thought about them, and the look on his face said it was a subject he would just as soon not discuss.

"In case you're wondering," he said, "I wasn't guilty. I didn't do what they said I did."

"I know you didn't. The jury found you innocent."

"There are some people who still think otherwise. It's damned hard to change people's minds. Especially around here."

"Murphy's in particular?"

Cole made a scoffing noise. "He's nothing but a narrow-minded old man."

Ginny wasn't quite sure about that. While Murphy was big and gruff and every bit as opinionated as Cole, it was easy to see that he really did have a good heart. So what was the problem between them?

"You never did tell me what brought you to this town when you were a teenager," she said.

"I came to stay with my grandmother."

"I know that. But why?"

"Just drop it, okay?"

"Hmm. You don't want to talk about it. That must mean the rumor I heard was true."

"What rumor?"

"That you killed someone during a gang war in Dallas and were hiding out at your grandmother's ranch until the heat was off."

"*What?*"

Ginny smiled. "That's what I heard, anyway."

"Good God," Cole said. "I can just imagine the stories they told about me when I was up on those arson charges."

Ginny picked up the remote and muted the sound. She turned to face him, eyeing him expectantly. Finally he sighed with resignation.

"When I was sixteen," he said, "my father got thrown in jail for writing one too many hot checks. My mother ran off years before that, so my grandmother took me in. I barely knew her, but she was the only family I had."

So that was it. No wonder Cole had a chip on his shoulder when he rode into town all those years ago. He'd come here with an attitude that said he didn't give a damn what anyone thought because he knew no one cared about him, either. She felt a rush of sympathy as one more piece of his puzzle fell into place.

"And then I met Murphy," Cole went on. "He hated me on sight. He naturally assumed that because of my father, I was bad news, too."

"Were you?"

"No. I mean, I guess I didn't exactly make things easy for them in the beginning, but I'm not my father, Ginny. I wasn't then, and I'm not now."

"So things were difficult between you and your grandmother?"

"No," he said sharply. "My grandmother was a wonderful person. It was Murphy. He was the problem. Men like him see things one way. Their way. He didn't give me the benefit of the doubt back then and he has no intention of doing it now, either. When the fire happened and I was investigated for arson, he took that to mean that he'd been right about me all along."

"But you were found innocent."

"He just figures I had a good lawyer."

"That's not fair. Murphy should give you a chance."

"Yes, he should."

"Maybe you should give him a chance, too."

Cole shrugged indifferently. "Actually, Ginny, none of this matters. I'll be out of here in a few months, and then we'll never have to see each other again."

He slipped the remote from her hand and turned up the volume, signaling that at least from his point of view, this particular conversation had come to a close.

The coldness she heard in his voice broke her heart. If his grandmother had been his only blood relative, that meant Murphy was the closest thing to family he had right now. That was such a precious thing to lose, and Cole didn't even realize it.

"Ginny, I'm telling you the job could be yours if only you'd apply for it."

Rhonda sat at the table in the tiny kitchen at the bank, flipping through the morning paper and chastising Ginny at the same time.

"Rhonda!" Ginny whispered. "It's a trainee position. Ruby is hardly going to give it to me. Not with Susan around."

"Susan has nothing on you."

"Oh, *please.*"

"I'm not kidding. You're smarter than Susan. You're more efficient than Susan. You're *nicer* than Susan."

"And Susan will be getting the job."

Rhonda huffed with disgust. "Do you really want Susan lording that over you from now on? Or would you rather be lording it over her?"

"I don't want to lord anything over anybody. And why aren't you applying for the job?"

"Me? With a panty-hose job? No way. I'm staying right

there behind the counter where I can go naked from the waist down if I want to. You, on the other hand, wear panty hose whether you have to or not. Now go after it."

Ginny wanted the job. That wasn't the question. She'd never wanted anything so badly in her life. But she didn't stand a chance, so why try? And since she'd be going to college soon anyway, what did it really matter in the long run?

"Darn," Rhonda said, stabbing her finger at the sports page. "I can't believe the Cowboys lost by only two points."

"It was that turnover in the fourth quarter," Ginny said. "They lost great field position."

Rhonda looked at her with astonishment. "I didn't know you were a football fan."

"I'm not. Or at least I wasn't. But Cole loves it. We watch football all the time. And you know, it's actually fairly interesting, once you know who all the players are."

"You know, Earl and I have been talking about getting tickets to a Cowboys home game. Why don't you two come along?"

Ginny stared at her. "All the way to Dallas?"

"Yeah. A road trip would be lots of fun."

A football game? In person?

"Maybe," she said. "Just tell me when you're planning to go, and I'll talk to Cole."

"Why don't we go this Sunday? The team's in town."

Ginny felt a tingle of excitement. Cole had said he'd once considered getting season tickets, so surely he'd want to go, wouldn't he?

11

COLE HADN'T BEEN too sure about making the two and a half hour trip into Dallas to see a Cowboys game. But Ginny's face had lit up when she'd asked him about it, so he didn't figure he could say no, particularly when he was the one who'd gotten her interested in the game in the first place.

Right now Ginny sat in the passenger seat of his Porsche, with Rhonda and Earl tucked into the tiny back seat. He'd warned them about the size of it, but Rhonda said his car would still be more fun than their Buick. Rhonda was a big-haired Texas girl with a twang that could have curdled milk. Her husband, Earl, was a corresponding Texas boy with a crew cut and a can of Skoal in his hip pocket, who talked loud and laughed hard, the kind of guy you felt as if you'd known forever even though you'd just met him.

As they headed down the state highway toward I-20, Ginny turned to Earl and Rhonda. "Is it a tight squeeze back there?"

"Oh, heck no," Rhonda said. "I've had sex in back seats smaller than this."

Earl turned to Rhonda with a perplexed expression. "You have?"

"Sure, honey. Now, don't go searching those memory banks of yours, because it wasn't with you."

"Oh." Earl shrugged. "Which is not to say we couldn't try it sometime."

Rhonda gave him a sly smile. "Think Cole might have something to say about that?"

"*Our* car, Rhonda."

"The Buick? What's the fun in that? It's twice the size of our bed."

"But at least the springs don't squeak."

Rhonda mulled that over for a moment. "True." She grinned. "Okay, honey, it's a date."

Ginny blushed a little, but still she laughed. And even though Cole would have sworn his two passengers would drive him nuts within half an hour, sooner or later their banter had him laughing right along with everyone else.

Rhonda scooted up and tapped Cole on the shoulder. "Did Virginia tell you about the job she's going to apply for?"

Ginny gave her a warning stare. "Rhonda—"

"It's a loan officer trainee position. Virginia's perfect for the job, but if she doesn't apply for it, it's going to go to Susan Barker. But Virginia's smarter than Susan, she's nicer to the customers, but she won't tell Ruby she wants it."

"Rhonda—"

"Cole. Tell her to do it. Tomorrow's the last day to apply. She wants the job. She just won't say so."

"Is that true, Ginny?"

"I'm really not qualified—"

"It's a trainee job!" Rhonda said. "There are no qualifications, except to be smart and to learn fast. And if Susan Barker gets it, I swear I'm burning that bank down."

"Hmm," Cole said. "Ginny and I will have to have a talk about that."

Ginny gave Rhonda a look of admonishment. "Thanks, Rhonda."

Rhonda sat back in her seat with a smug grin. "You're welcome." Then her eyebrows flew up. "Wait a minute. Did I hear Cole call you Ginny?"

"Uh, yeah."

"Well, I like that a whole lot better than Virginia." She smiled. "Ginny it is."

WHEN THEY ENTERED Texas Stadium, Ginny simply could not believe her eyes.

"I've never seen so many people in one place before," she told Cole. "Everybody in the city of Dallas must be here!"

"Not quite, sweetheart. But it looks like a good portion of them, doesn't it?"

They found their seats, which were pretty good ones on the thirty-yard line. It was cool without being cold, and the light sweater Ginny wore was just enough to keep her cozily warm. The whole stadium seemed to be in motion, with people milling around, cheering at pregame activity and running up and down the stairs for hot dogs and sodas and a variety of other junk food guaranteed to stop up your arteries. It was one thing to watch a game on television. It was another thing entirely to see it in person, and she couldn't stop smiling.

Ginny leaned over and whispered to Cole. "Thanks for coming."

"You really didn't have to twist my arm to come to a football game."

"Thanks just the same."

She smiled at him and he smiled back, and she knew for a fact that this was going to be one of the best afternoons of her life.

They cheered themselves hoarse through the first half, at which point the Cowboys were up by only a field goal. As the teams headed for their respective locker rooms, Earl and Rhonda offered to get sodas for everybody. After they disappeared down the steps, Cole turned to Ginny.

"The job Rhonda was talking about," he said. "Apply for it."

"Cole—"

"Stop hiding your head in the sand around that place. You're better than you think you are. Don't you dare let somebody else have a job that ought to be yours."

"You know our situation. I wouldn't be keeping the job long."

"That's not the point. You've spent your whole life being afraid of things. It's time you stopped that. If you're the best candidate for that job, tell your supervisor so, and don't take no for an answer."

Ginny stared at Cole with surprise. He had a way of spelling things out in simple, direct terms until they didn't seem so scary, after all. All at once she had the same feeling she'd had the night they'd talked about her mother—the feeling that her life didn't have to stay the same as it had always been. She could grow. She could do better. She could have more, if only she made the decision to go after it.

"Okay," she told him, feeling a surge of self-confidence. "Maybe I will."

"Of course you will," Cole said, as if the issue had already been decided. "Now, tell me what you think is wrong with the Cowboys' offense today."

"I don't know. Maybe the three-hundred-pound guys on the other team's defensive line are kind of getting in their way."

Cole laughed. "Yeah, that just might have something to do with it."

"Why, Cole McCallum! Long time no see!"

Cole looked up to see a woman standing beside him, with long, dark hair, excessive makeup and generous breasts tucked inside a too-tight T-shirt. He had the feeling he ought to know who she was, but her name escaped him.

"Janet Lupinsky," she said, smiling seductively. "Surely you remember me, don't you?"

He thought he did. Maybe. Vaguely. "Sure, Janet," he said, giving her a generic smile in return. "How are you?"

"Better now," she said, purring and plunking herself into the empty seat beside him. "Why, I had no idea we'd be running into each other. Can you believe the luck?"

Yeah, Cole thought. *Lucky me.*

"Hey, I heard about the arson thing," she said with an expression of mock sympathy. "Too bad. Hear you got off, though." She sidled closer to him. "How would you like to get off again?"

Cole raised an eyebrow. "Excuse me?"

"After the game," she replied, "we can find ourselves a nice little hotel room and let whatever comes...come. It'd be kind of like old times."

"Sorry, I can't do that."

"Why, sure you can, sugar. In fact," she said, easing closer still, "you can do it better than just about any man I know."

"Sorry, Janet. I'm a married man."

She drew back with a look of total shock. "Cole McCallum? *Married?*" She laughed. "You're kidding me, right?"

"Never been more serious."

"Well," she said, turning her seductive smile on, "don't let a little thing like that stop you. After all, what your wife doesn't know won't hurt her."

"It will if she's sitting right next to him," Ginny said.

The woman froze, then slowly turned her gaze in Ginny's direction, her face filled with flagrant disbelief.

"You? You're his *wife?*"

She held out her hand and gave Janet a great big smile. "Ginny McCallum. It's a pleasure to meet you."

The woman shook her hand dumbly. She stared back and forth between them for a full five seconds, blinking as if she couldn't possibly comprehend what her eyes were telling her.

"Can I give you a little advice, Janet?" Ginny said.

"Uh, what?"

Ginny rested her palm on Cole's thigh, leaned across him and motioned the woman closer. "If a man says he's married and there's a woman sitting right next to him...well, next time you might want to make that mental leap and kind of put the two things together. Okay, Janet?"

Cole couldn't believe it. Had those words actually come out of Ginny's mouth?

She continued to smile sweetly, while Janet looked a little bit nauseated. Finally she mumbled something that sounded like an apology and slunk away.

"I'm sorry about that, Ginny," Cole said. "She's just some bimbo I knew once."

"Forget it. It's no big deal."

"She's got a lot of nerve to sit there and say all those things right in front of you."

"Don't worry about it."

"I mean it. Don't listen to anything a woman like that says. She's nothing but a—"

"Cole, will you hush? The wave's coming!"

For at least the tenth time that day, people leaped out of their seats and threw their arms in the air, doing their part to send an undulating wave of bodies in motion all the way around the stadium. Ginny leaped up right along with them. He stared at her with disbelief. Was this the same woman who ran from her own shadow only a few months ago?

"You enjoyed that, didn't you?" he said, as she sat down.

"Of course I did. There's nothing like a really good wave to get your blood rushing."

"You know what I mean."

Ginny twisted her mouth with disgust. "She deserved it. I don't like women who go after married men."

He smiled. "Especially when you're married to the man she's going after?"

Her face fell. "Don't tease me, Cole."

"I'm not teasing you, sweetheart. Believe me. I like a woman who stands up for herself." Cole slipped his arm along the top of her chair behind her back and leaned in closer to her. "I like it a lot."

He couldn't help it. Watching Ginny put that woman in her place did something to him that he just couldn't describe. And as he looked at her now, something seemed to come alive between them, something new and different that had never been there before.

He dropped his hand to her shoulder and pulled her gently toward him. She yielded to the pressure, moving closer. He brought his other hand up, touching her cheek with his fingertips. She didn't look away, she didn't blush, she didn't remind him of any rule she'd made that he was in the process of breaking. Instead she put her hand against his shoulder, then slid it slowly to his neck, where her fingertips met his bare skin.

"You're really something special, Ginny. Don't you ever settle for less than you deserve, do you hear me?"

He lowered his mouth toward hers. The crowd roared suddenly at something going on down on the field, but Cole scarcely heard it. It was as if all the sights and sounds around him had blurred into nothingness, and all he knew on this earth was Ginny's thumb moving softly against his neck and his lips hovering only an inch away from hers.

"Newlyweds. Look at 'em, Rhonda. It's downright nauseating!"

Ginny pulled away suddenly, and Cole looked around to see Rhonda give Earl an elbow to the ribs for his rowdy comment. Then Rhonda turned to Ginny. "He'll be looking to get nauseating himself before the day's out, believe me."

Earl rolled his eyes and plopped down beside Rhonda, then doled out the sodas. After a moment, Cole reached over and took Ginny's hand in his. He held it through most of the rest of the game, with a little squeeze here and there to remind her of their unfinished business. She never pulled away, and every once in a while she'd look over, their eyes would meet, and he'd know that they were thinking the same thing.

Rhonda prattled on at Ginny, something about the Coldwater Booster Club she was a member of. They did things such as running the concession stand at games and having bake sales to raise money for the sports teams at the high school. Since Ginny liked football, Rhonda asked her if maybe she'd like to come along sometime and help out. It was fun, she said, since mostly it was the moms of the athletes and the female alumni of Coldwater High who participated, and they did as much yakking as they did working. Ginny smiled and said that she would love to join them, but Cole could tell her mind really was somewhere else.

By the time the game was over and they left the stadium, Cole was so consumed with getting home that he couldn't have stated the final score if his life depended on it. He had no idea how far this would go. He only knew that for the first time in his life he didn't want sex just for the sake of sex. The woman he wanted to make love to wasn't some nebulous beauty queen with a gorgeous but generic body whose name he wouldn't even remember in the morning.

She was beside him right now. And her name was Ginny.

As COLE and Ginny drove through the darkened gates of the ranch, her heart raced with anticipation. Ever since they'd dropped Rhonda and Earl off at their house, neither she nor Cole had said a word, and the silence was deafening.

For all her protesting in the past, she wanted desperately to feel his lips against hers again, his arms embracing her and see that look in his eyes that said he wanted her. The sensation was so powerful she almost couldn't contain it. Almost every night after he'd gone to sleep, she stared at him, imagining what it would be like to reach across the short distance that separated them and touch his cheek, stroke his shoulder until he woke up, then tell him how foolish she'd been, and that of course she wanted him to make love to her.

But that was fantasy. Tonight was reality.

Until a few months ago, the monotony of her life had dulled her senses to the point where she'd rarely felt anything. Then she'd met Cole, and he'd yanked her emotions from one end of the spectrum to the other. He made her think about things in ways she'd never thought about them before, made her *feel* things she'd never felt before, whether anger or fear...or sexual attraction. But no matter how much she wanted him, she knew in her heart that making love with Cole would be just about the most dangerous thing she could possibly do.

They came into the kitchen, and Ginny quickly turned on the overhead light, which cast a bright, comforting glow around the room. She set her purse on the counter.

Cole came up beside her. She could practically feel the heat radiating from his body, and the tiny trace of comfort she'd felt evaporated.

"It's late," she said. "I'm tired. I—I guess I'll go get ready for bed."

Bed. Oh, Lord—that was the *last* place she needed to be with Cole.

She slipped away from him, grabbed a pair of pajamas from the dresser in the bedroom, then headed for the bathroom, where she flipped on the light and closed the door behind her.

How was she ever going to go into that bedroom and sleep with him tonight? She sensed that the moment she lay down beside him he would pull her into his arms, and she wanted it so much. But she also knew the possible consequences, and she wasn't anywhere near ready to face those.

She changed into her pajamas and brushed her teeth, then stared at herself in the mirror, wondering what to do next. She couldn't stay in here forever. Sooner or later she was going to have to face him. She would have to look into those deep, dark eyes of his and tell him no when she wanted so desperately to say yes.

She took a deep breath, then opened the door.

Cole was waiting for her.

12

COLE WALKED slowly into the bathroom. With every step he took forward, Ginny took one step backward, until she bumped into the counter. She turned her back to him, her heart beating crazily.

Then he turned out the bathroom light, leaving only the hazy light from the hall to illuminate the tiny room.

Oh, God.

He moved up behind her and closed his hands over her upper arms, caressing her from her shoulders to her elbows. He eased the length of his body against hers, then dipped his head until his breath spilled over her ear.

"I got cheated out of a kiss today."

Ginny felt a surge of panic. It was one thing for Cole to kiss her in front of sixty thousand people, where he could do nothing *but* kiss her. It was another thing entirely to do it when they were alone in the dark.

"Cole—"

"No," he said softly, standing behind her, his breath warm against her ear. "Don't say anything. Just listen to me."

She met his dark-eyed gaze in the mirror. The dim light from the hall, along with the moonlight streaking in through the window, offered just enough illumination that she could make out his face, but it wasn't nearly enough to take away her apprehension.

"In the beginning I pressured you because I wanted to have sex," Cole said. "That's all I was after. I'm not proud of that, but it's the truth. But lately..." He tightened his hands against her shoulders. "If I was just looking for sex, I'd have found it somewhere else by now. It's not just sex with any woman I want, Ginny. I want to make love. With you."

She knew he was telling the truth. Something had changed between them. She'd felt it today at the game just as she felt it now. But still, she felt so tense she trembled.

"Ginny?" he whispered. "Why are you so afraid of this?"

"I'm not afraid. I just don't want—"

"No. Don't say you don't want it. That's a lie."

She squeezed her eyes closed. "Cole—"

"I can see it in your eyes every day. I can feel it when we're in bed together at night. And today— Oh, Ginny. Please don't lie to me anymore. It's too easy to see the truth."

He was right. To say she didn't want it was a lie, but she *was* afraid.

She was afraid that she would be so inept she would disappoint him. She was afraid she would be embarrassed by her lack of a really nice lingerie wardrobe. She was afraid of what her body would look like to him naked. Most of all, she was afraid that a few moments of pleasure would lead to a lifetime of responsibility. Responsibility she would have to face by herself. He'd already made it quite clear that he would be gone at the end of six months. He was already making plans for it, wasn't he?

"I don't want to push you into anything," he said. "I swear I won't do that. We've argued about it, we've yelled about it and we've ignored it. But we've never just talked about it."

She met his gaze in the mirror. His eyes shimmered in the moonlight, not seductively, but tenderly, and the sight of it went straight to her heart.

"It does scare me," she admitted. "For a lot of reasons. But mostly because I'm afraid of..."

"Of what?"

"Pregnancy," she whispered.

He recoiled slightly. "Is that all?"

"Is that *all?*"

"I have protection, Ginny. It's not a problem."

"It's not a hundred percent effective."

"Nothing in this life is a hundred percent."

Ginny sighed. "I've wanted this for a long time, Cole. Even when I said I didn't." She let out a small, humorless laugh. "I'm not even exactly sure what *it* involves, and I know it must be wonderful, but when I think of the possible consequences..." She sighed again. "I just can't take that chance."

He opened his mouth to speak, then stopped and met her eyes in the mirror. She could sense him trying to find the words to counter her argument, but he didn't voice any of them. Instead, he leaned in and dropped a gentle kiss against her neck.

"Then we won't do anything that involves taking a chance."

She felt momentary relief, right up to the second he slid his hands across her shoulders and closed his fingers around the top button of her pajamas.

"What are you doing?"

He flicked the button open. Stunned, she reached up, intending to stop him, but he took her wrists and pushed her hands gently down again.

"No," he whispered. "Don't move."

"I told you I can't do this."

"As long as it's just my hands," he said, easing them up to her buttons, "and my lips," he whispered, teasing them along her cheek, "there's nothing to worry about."

"Cole—"

"It's okay, sweetheart. I heard what you said. Every word." She let out a shaky sigh.

"Just touching, Ginny. That's all. And I swear I'll stop anytime you say."

She should have stopped him, but how could she, when all she'd been able to think about all day was what it would feel like if he touched her again? And how could she say no when, against all odds, she'd come to trust him so much?

He moved his hands to open the next button, then the next. She was mesmerized by the reflection of his big, strong hands in the mirror, deftly flicking the buttons open. When he reached the last one, he traced his fingertip all the way up the opening, along her abdomen, in the hollow between her breasts and finally to her collarbone. Then slowly he pulled the sides of the shirt apart, exposing her breasts. Ginny felt a surge of panic.

She'd never been naked in front of a man before. Never. The vulnerability she felt was so overpowering it was all she could do not to yank her pajama top shut. "Cole—"

"Shh," he whispered against her ear, cradling her breasts with his palms, his thumbs lightly stroking them.

She closed her eyes. "Please. This is *so* embarrassing."

"No," he said, his voice a husky whisper. "Believe me, sweetheart. You've got nothing to be embarrassed about."

He closed his hands over her breasts, squeezing softly, then swept his thumbs across her nipples. She shifted against him, the feeling so intense she wanted to beg him to stop, but at the same time it felt so good that she *never* wanted him to stop.

"Open your eyes," he said.

She eased her eyes open and stared into the mirror. In the midst of all her self-consciousness, she felt a tiny thrill deep inside. Cole was staring at her, seemingly transfixed, looking at her in a way no man had ever looked at her before.

With desire.

"You're beautiful," he whispered.

"No."

"Oh, yes," he said. *"Beautiful."*

He flattened one palm just below her breasts, then skimmed it down over her abdomen. She sighed softly and rested her head against his shoulder, her eyes falling closed again. When his hand reached the barrier of her pajama bottoms, he slid it beneath the elastic waistband. She tensed, shocked at the sudden invasion, and before she knew it, he'd slipped his hand beneath her panties and tangled his fingers in the curls at the apex of her thighs.

She gasped.

He shifted his hand lower still, touching a place so sensitive it shocked her. She gasped again and took hold of his wrist to still his hand.

"Relax, sweetheart," he whispered. "Let me touch you."

"I can't, Cole. I can't. It feels—"

"Just a minute more. Then you can tell me all about how it feels."

He began to stroke her there, slowly, rhythmically, and at the same time he caressed her breasts with his other hand. He whispered nothing words against her ear, sounds that were soothing and comforting and endlessly erotic all at the same time, interspersed with warm kisses on her cheek, her neck, her shoulder. In all her ignorance, she'd never imagined a man touching her like this, and it took her breath away.

But it wasn't just the heavenly feeling of his hands on her. Something was happening deep inside her—a powerful sensation that was building slowly, giving her a sense of edginess and impatience. She leaned against Cole as the hot, hazy feelings swept through her. She breathed faster, more erratically, and before long the feeling had grown almost unbearable.

What was he *doing* to her?

As much as she'd wanted him to stop before, that was how desperately she wanted him to continue now. She found herself moving along with his strokes because it was impossible not to, all the while feeling as if she was reaching for something just beyond her grasp, so crazed with some indescribable need that she was on the verge of begging him to do *any-thing* to take the tension away.

"Tell me now, sweetheart," he murmured. "How does it feel?"

"It feels...oh, Cole—"

For a second, maybe two, she had a sense that the world had come to a standstill. Then something inside her shattered, and a blinding white heat raced through her that was so intense her knees buckled. Cole's arms encircled her, holding her close, and she clamped her hand onto his arm and held on tightly as waves of indescribable pleasure rushed through her. The intense, insistent pulsing between her legs fanned out to become a heavy, throbbing rhythm throughout the rest of her body, encompassing every nerve ending, sending her heart into such an incredible overload that she felt as if she was on the verge of passing out.

Slowly, slowly the feeling subsided. Her muscles, so tense before, became suddenly weak and helpless. She exhaled softly, then fell limp against him.

And Cole felt as if he was going to explode.

He tucked his chin into the crook of her neck. Closing his eyes, he took a deep, ragged breath, trying to ignore the fact that she was pressed so tightly against his groin that even the tiniest shift of her body sent currents of electricity racing through him.

He wanted her desperately, so desperately he almost forgot that she trusted him to touch her without demanding more, even though he wanted all of her. *Now.*

And he couldn't have her. Why in the hell had he even started this if he couldn't finish it?

Because he'd wanted to hear her cry out. Wanted to feel her

dissolve in his arms. Wanted to be the first to touch her and make her feel those things when a man had never touched her before.

He turned her around to face him. She looked at him, those languid brown eyes still glazed with pleasure, and it took every bit of self-control he had to pull the sides of her shirt together and button it, to watch with regret as her beautiful breasts disappeared from his view.

He swept her into his arms and carried her into the bedroom. He laid her on the bed, her head on the pillow, then sat beside her.

She slid her hand into his. "That was..." Her voice trailed off, her chest still heaving gently. "I don't know what to say."

He brushed a damp strand of hair from her cheek, and suddenly he imagined her, somewhere down the line, in the arms of another man—a man who would take that part of her innocence she could only give once. Would he treat her gently? Or would he take what he wanted with no concern for her at all?

When Cole realized what the answer to those questions might be, he wanted desperately to show her how wonderful the whole gamut of lovemaking could be so she would never settle for anything less.

If only she would let him.

"Just promise me something, Ginny."

"What?"

"Whenever you decide you want a man to make love to you for the first time...I want it to be me."

She smiled softly. "Didn't we kind of just do that?"

"Yes," he murmured. "But there's more."

"I know." She stroked his thigh, staring boldly at his erection still straining against his jeans, and he just about lost it right there. Then she shifted her gaze to meet his.

"I want it to be you, too."

Dead silence. Cole didn't move, didn't breathe. "When?"

"I just have to be more sure—"

"Sure?"

"About birth control."

Cole took a deep breath and let it out slowly. "Okay. So...what do you want to do?"

"I'll see a doctor."

"The pill?"

"I've read about it in magazines. It's the most effective thing. But we'll have to wait at least a month."

Cole had never heard such an incredible case of good news, bad news in his entire life. Good God, could he wait a month?

"Okay," he said, staring at her.

She lay there like an angel, her hair fanned out on the pillow and her cheeks flushed pink, and he wanted her so badly he could taste it.

Leave. Right now.

He started to move away. She took hold of his wrist.

"Cole?" she murmured. "Where are you going?"

"The sofa."

"No," she said sleepily. "Stay."

She didn't know what she was asking. If he stayed, he'd take her, so hard, so hot and so fast that she wouldn't even realize what had happened until it was all over.

He was *never* going to last a month. He was going to see her every day, want her every day, and every kiss he gave her, every touch, every whisper of a caress would lead to—

"For the next month," he said, "no touching."

"Didn't we just abolish that rule?"

"Yeah, and it just about killed me." He took a deep breath and let it out slowly. "I'm sorry, Ginny. But I've got to have all or nothing."

She looked at him with astonishment. "So...nothing?"

"That's right. And I'm going to sleep on the sofa."

"That's silly."

"For the next month."

"That's even sillier."

"Sorry, that's the way it's got to be. Good night, Ginny."

He kissed her forehead, pulled the blankets carefully over her, then stood up. He grabbed a blanket and pillow from the closet.

"I'll miss you," she murmured sleepily as he walked out the door, and he had to resist the urge to go running back in.

He went to the sofa, tossed down the blanket and pillow, then tossed himself down on top of them and tried vainly to get comfortable. He couldn't.

I'll miss you, too, Ginny. More than you can possibly imagine.

THE MOMENT Ginny got to work the next morning, she told Ruby she wanted to talk to her about the loan officer trainee position, and Ruby immediately summoned her to her office. Ginny sat down in the chair in front of her boss's desk, her palms sweaty, her throat so dry she didn't know if she was even going to be able to speak, not to mention the fact that she couldn't get last night's experience with Cole out of her mind. The odds of her being coherent enough to make a good impression were pretty slim, but she had no choice. This was the last day to apply for the job, and Ruby was a stickler for schedules.

"So," Ruby said, as she took her seat behind her desk. "You're interested in the loan officer trainee position."

"Yes," Ginny said, clearing her throat. "Yes, I am."

"This is going to be a very simple interview, Virginia."

Thank goodness, Ginny thought, knowing she couldn't possibly think straight enough to do a complicated one.

Ruby leaned back, her elbows on the armrests of her chair and her fingers steepled in front of her.

"Tell me why you think you should have this job."

Oh, boy, Ginny thought. *One of those awful open-ended questions that's so easy to goof up.*

She sat up straighter, took a deep, silent breath and tried her best to come off confident and professional.

"I've worked at this bank for six years," Ginny began. "My performance evaluations have always been exemplary. I enjoy working as a teller, but I've learned all I can in that position, and I'm ready to move on. I have a good basic understanding of banking, but I know there's so much more that I can learn if I'm allowed to move up. I have an excellent rapport with many of the customers, and I know I could translate that into more business for the bank if I became a loan officer."

Ruby stared at her, those dark brows of hers drawn together, and Ginny felt a flood of apprehension.

"Anything else?" Ruby said.

Ginny heard Cole's words playing over and over in her head. *You're something special, Ginny. Don't you settle for less than what you deserve, do you hear me?*

"Yes, Ruby. There's no question in my mind that I'm the best candidate for the job. And knowing me as you do, there should be no question in yours, either."

Ruby lifted her eyebrows, little creases forming in her forehead. "Those are pretty powerful words, Virginia."

Ginny felt the challenge in Ruby's words, but she couldn't back down now. "Yes, they are. And I mean every one of them."

Ginny's heart was beating so rapidly that she started to wonder just exactly what a heart attack felt like. Ruby continued to stare at her with that intense, assessing expression. Finally she leaned forward and folded her hands on her desk.

"To tell you the truth, Virginia, you were the first person I thought of when this position was created, but I was only going to consider candidates who expressed interest. When you didn't seem inclined to apply for it, I assumed you didn't want it."

Ginny felt a stab of disappointment. She'd waited too long. She'd waited too long, and now—

"But since you do appear to want it," Ruby said, "the job is yours."

Ginny blinked with astonishment. "What did you say?"

"I said the job is yours. Go see Alice about the change in job title. You'll start as soon as we can hire another teller. Now, don't think you're getting a salary increase. This is a trainee position. But I expect you'll move quickly through that, and when you have the position officially, we'll talk about a raise."

"Uh...yeah. Okay."

Ginny continued to stare at Ruby, still certain she couldn't possibly have heard her right.

"Virginia," Ruby said slowly, carefully. "The interview is over. You got the job. Now go."

Ginny rose, thanking Ruby at the same time, then walked to her teller window in a daze.

"So tell me," Rhonda whispered. "What happened?"

Ginny looked at her, still dumbfounded. "I got the job."

Rhonda whooped. "Oh, sweetie, I *knew* you could do it!"

Out of the corner of her eye, Ginny saw Susan giving them both the evil eye. She must have surmised what happened, because she circled her desk and flounced her way into Ruby's office, slamming the door behind her. Ginny heard a lot of muffled shouts, and when Susan finally emerged again, she went to her desk, grabbed her purse and stormed out of the bank.

"My, my," Rhonda said innocently. "She seems a little miffed. Ginny, does she seem a little miffed to you?"

Ginny was going to have to leave the vengeful remarks to

Rhonda, because right now there was only one thing she could think about.

I got the job. And I can't wait to tell Cole.

COLE CAME HOME that night all hot and sweaty from working on the ranch, so he was shocked when he opened the kitchen door and Ginny launched herself into his arms.

He hugged her automatically, but given how he looked and smelled right about now, he was sure she was going to regret it.

"Cole, I got it! I got the job!"

He took her by the shoulders. "The trainee job? You got it?"

"Yes! Ruby said I was the first person she thought of, but since I didn't apply, she thought I didn't want it. Then, when I told her I did, she gave it to me. On the spot!"

Cole pulled her into his arms in a gigantic bear hug. "I knew you would get it!"

"I didn't," she said. "Not until you told me I could."

She gave him a quick kiss on the cheek, then laid her palm against the spot where she'd kissed him.

"Thank you, Cole."

He smiled. "I want you to give me all the details over dinner."

"I will. Take a quick shower, and it'll be ready in a few minutes."

Cole headed for the bathroom, listening to Ginny hum while she cooked, and he had the oddest feeling inside, a strange sense of accomplishment, even though she was the one who'd gotten the job.

But you helped her do it.

For all the years he'd invested in real estate, each contract bigger than the last, he couldn't remember a deal he'd made that had satisfied him more than Ginny's news had tonight.

He was halfway down the hall when Ginny called to him again.

"Cole? One more thing."

He stepped to the kitchen doorway. "Yeah?"

"I went to the doctor today."

"Oh?"

"He gave me a prescription and told me the third Friday in October would be all right."

She gave him a tiny smile, then turned to her cooking, as if she'd just mentioned the date of a dental appointment or an oil change.

The third Friday in October.

That hot shower he was anticipating had, by necessity, just become a cold one.

13

THE NEXT MONTH was the longest of Cole's life.

Every move Ginny made drove him crazy. She couldn't even bend over to take a pan out of the oven without him thinking about her being naked. Wearing the apron, maybe. Only the apron.

Some evenings she'd go with Rhonda to meet with the women of the Coldwater Booster Club, and she always came home in a good mood, chattering about whatever project they were working on at the time. He knew Ginny had had very little social life before now, and getting out with other women made her positively glow with excitement, which made him want her that much more. It got so ridiculous that after a while she could get him excited just by brushing her teeth.

Then she talked him into going riding with her, and damned if that didn't shake him up, too.

She must have really studied the ads in *Western Horseman*, because somewhere along the way she'd bought a couple of pairs of blue jeans that fit. *Really* fit. And every time he watched her walk away, his mind wandered places he really wished it wouldn't go, especially since the rest of his body wasn't invited.

But other than Cole's almost debilitating preoccupation with the prospect of making love to Ginny, the month passed uneventfully. The ranch was alive with fall colors, and on the weekends he and Ginny rode in the midst of them, sometimes for hours. Cole found enjoyment in riding a horse for the first time, though he was coming to realize that just about anything he did with Ginny he enjoyed.

He was glad, though, that he'd instituted the no-touching rule, because it seemed as if most of the time when they were at the barn, Murphy's eyes were on them, and he didn't appear to like what he saw. Even though it was none of the old man's business what was going on between them, Cole knew he was passing judgment—always passing judgment—and Cole had already had enough of that to last him a lifetime.

When that Friday finally came, Cole was dismayed when Murphy asked him, in the middle of the afternoon, to ride out to one of the far pastures in search of a yearling who hadn't come in with the rest of the herd. Cole eventually found her deep in the fifty wooded acres at the back of the property, with no clue as to why she'd wandered off. After a cat-and-mouse game that lasted a good thirty minutes with Cole cussing the filly the whole time, he finally got a halter on her to lead her home.

He checked his watch. Five o'clock.

It would take him a while to ride back in, and by the time he finished up around the barn, it was going to be after six. Ginny would be home already. Waiting for him.

Once he got home, he'd need a shower first, but maybe he could persuade Ginny that she needed one, too. At the same time. He shifted uncomfortably in the saddle at the prospect of seeing her naked and wet, and he decided that would definitely have to be on the agenda for tonight.

When the time finally came for Cole to head home, anticipation had every single nerve in his body humming. As he approached the house, though, he noticed Ginny's car wasn't out front. He went inside and was met with total quiet. He called for her. Nothing.

Where was she?

Then he saw the note on the kitchen table, and when he realized what it said, he thought he was going to explode.

She'd gone to Rhonda's house to bake cookies for a Coldwater Booster Club bake sale. And she wouldn't be home for *hours*.

Cole crumpled the note, every muscle in his body tied into a tight knot of frustration. He couldn't believe it. They'd planned on making love for the first time tonight, and she was baking cookies?

No. No way. She was coming home, and she was coming home *now*.

He tossed the note aside and reached for the telephone.

GINNY HAD just put another pan of cookies into Rhonda's oven when the phone rang. Rhonda picked it up and her eyes widened.

"Just a minute, Cole. I'll get her."

The moment Rhonda said Cole's name, Loretta and Darlene, who were sitting at the kitchen table, immediately stopped their conversation and whipped their heads around.

Rhonda held out the phone to Ginny. "Look out," she whispered. "He sounds a little unhappy."

Ginny took the phone. "Hello?"

"What are you doing?" Cole snapped.

Ginny smiled. "I guess you got the note I left."

"Yeah. I saw the note. Forget the cookies. Come home."

"I'm sorry, Cole. I have to do this. We realized we're going to need more cookies than we thought, so it's kind of an emergency. I'll be home when we're finished."

"No. Come home *now*."

The urgency in his voice thrilled her. She hadn't done this on purpose, but it was certainly turning into something interesting just the same.

"Ginny?" he said sharply. "Did you hear me? Come home *right now.*"

"Well, now," she said, stepping away from the other women and lowering her voice. "We're getting a little bossy, aren't we?"

She heard him take a deep, calming breath and let it out slowly, his tone perceptibly shifting. "No, sweetheart. No. Now, you know I don't mean to be bossy. But we had plans tonight, didn't we?"

"Of course. They're just delayed a little. That's all."

"How long will you be?"

"I don't know. Three hours. Maybe four."

"Four hours?"

"It takes a while to bake forty dozen cookies."

"Forty dozen?"

"Just relax, Cole," she said, hugging the phone to her ear, excitement tingling all the way down to her toes. "Have a little dinner. Watch a little TV. I'll be home before you know it."

She hung up the phone over the sound of him protesting one more time, smiling to herself, wishing in a way that she could rush right home and leap into his arms, but she really did have to help bake these cookies. Besides, there was something about him wanting her home so badly that sent warmth spreading through her like kindling catching fire.

She sat at the kitchen table with Rhonda and the other women.

"Everything okay?" Rhonda asked. "He sounded a little hot under the collar."

"Oh, he'll be fine before the night is out. Believe me."

The women exchanged glances, then looked at Ginny.

"He's just a little frustrated that I'm not home right now," Ginny added. "This was going to be, well...a special night for us."

In unison, the women raised their eyebrows.

"Just the two of us," Ginny went on, wearing a tiny smile. "You know."

"That's it!" Loretta said, waving her hand wildly. "I can't stand it anymore!" She looked at Ginny, an earnest expression on her face. "You've got to tell us, Ginny. You're a really cute girl and all, so don't get me wrong, but I never would have thought that Cole McCallum would settle down with *anyone*, and here he is setting up housekeeping with you on that ranch like some kind of family man." She inched closer, dropping her voice. "So what's your secret?"

Darlene and Rhonda leaned in, too, and silence fell over the kitchen. Ginny couldn't believe it. Loretta and Darlene had been two years ahead of her in high school, both popular girls who'd had plenty of dates. She was the last person they'd have asked for advice about boys, yet here they were now, waiting for her to enlighten them on man-woman relationships.

"Well," she said, treading the line between truth and fiction very lightly, "I suppose the secret is to give a man *exactly* what he needs."

Eyes widened like searchlights all around the table. But Ginny hadn't lied. Cole had needed a wife for six months, and she'd provided him one.

"So tell us, then." Loretta prodded her. "Exactly what does a man like Cole McCallum need?"

"Loretta!" Rhonda said. "That's none of your business!"

"Shoot, Rhonda! It's just girl talk! I've been trying to get Billy to pop the question for two years now. Ginny got Cole to marry her in two days. I was hoping maybe she could give me a few pointers!"

"It's still none of your business, so keep your questions to yourself," Rhonda scolded. She paused a moment, then turned and eyed Ginny carefully. "Unless Ginny *wants* to tell us, of course."

From the hopeful look on her friend's face, Ginny knew her sudden marriage had been driving Rhonda just as crazy as everyone else. She'd just had the good grace not to pressure her into talking about it.

Ginny smiled. "Who can tell what brings two people together? It was just...one of those things."

Loretta sat back in her chair, folding her arms over her chest with disgust. "Yeah, right. Don't tell me you don't know something the rest of us don't, Ginny, because I'm not believing it."

"Cole's just got the good sense to recognize a really fine woman when he meets one," Rhonda said. "Case closed. Now, get another couple batches of cookies ready to go in or we'll be here all night."

Everyone went back to plunking cookie dough onto the cookie sheets, and after a while the oven timer went off, signaling that another batch was done. Ginny hopped up to take it out of the oven when she heard a loud rap, then three more loud, very insistent ones, on the front door.

The women fell silent, looking at each other quizzically.

"Who on earth could that be?" Rhonda said, walking warily to the door as the rest of them followed her out of the kitchen. She looked out the peephole, then spun around.

"Ginny!" she whispered. "It's Cole!"

Ginny's heart skittered crazily. Cole knocked again, even harder.

"He looks kind of mad," Rhonda whispered. "Sure you want me to let him in?"

Ginny smiled. "He's only going to get angrier if you don't," she whispered.

Rhonda opened the door, and Cole strode across the threshold. "Where's Ginny?"

His gaze swept around the room. When it finally landed on Ginny, she felt warmth puddling in her stomach—and lower.

She couldn't resist. She crossed her arms over her chest and gave him a sweet little smile, and for a moment she truly thought he was going to stalk across the room like some kind of chest-beating Neanderthal, sling her over his shoulder and drag her kicking and screaming to his cave.

He walked over to her slowly, his expression growing more intense with every step he took. He stopped in front of her, and for a moment it appeared as if the Neanderthal thing was a real possibility.

Ginny gave him an innocent smile. "The cookies are for a very good cause," she whispered.

"I'll get you for this later," he whispered.

"Is that a promise?"

"Oh, you can bet on it, sweetheart."

Ginny loved the sound of his voice—deep and provocative and very, *very* impatient.

He inched closer to her. "Are you trying to tell me you don't intend to come home until those cookies are baked?"

"I'm afraid so."

He took a deep breath and let it out slowly. "Well, then. I guess there's only one thing I can do."

He turned to face the other women, sweeping his gaze over them with the intensity of a Marine sergeant reviewing his troops before going into battle.

"Okay, ladies. I hear we've got forty dozen cookies to bake. Let's get with it."

The women might have fainted dead away, except that Cole got them moving to the point where falling down on the job wasn't an option. Within minutes, he'd instructed Rhonda to pull out every bowl she had in the kitchen, lined the women up along the counter and started calling out ingredients and amounts. They measured and stirred with speed and precision, and all the while Cole urged them on, picking up the biggest bowl himself and stirring when things weren't moving quite fast enough for him.

"Now, see how much more efficient that is?" he said with a big smile, brushing flour off his hands.

The women nodded, looking a little shell-shocked.

"You have double ovens," he said to Rhonda. "Why aren't you using the other one?"

"It doesn't work. But since it's just Earl and me, we don't need it, so I never bothered to get it fixed."

Cole yanked open the door and peered deep inside. "Well, look at that. It's just your pilot light. I'll have that fixed in a jiffy."

He appropriated some matches from Rhonda and lit the pilot light, and pretty soon they had two ovens full of cookies going at the same time.

"So what's up with Cole?" Rhonda whispered to Ginny. "He's not exactly the cookie-baking type."

"He just wants to help out. That's all."

"Oh, yeah. Like Earl wants to crochet doilies and paint my toenails. So what's up?"

Ginny smiled at her.

"I'll get it out of you sooner or later," Rhonda warned. "You see if I don't."

Once Rhonda's back was turned, Ginny caught Cole's eye, then slyly stuck her finger into the dough, bringing a fingerful out of the bowl and licking it off very slowly. She'd seen a woman do something like that in a movie once, and it drove her boyfriend wild. Sure enough, Cole followed every furtive flick of her tongue, then spun around and asked Darlene why in the world she was putting only twelve cookies on one of the sheets when fifteen would *clearly* fit.

Later, Ginny stepped down the hall to the bathroom. When she came out, a hand clamped onto her arm. Cole pulled her against him in the darkened hall, his hands sliding down to her hips and up again, then moving to cradle her face. Then he kissed her for the first time in a month, and suddenly cookie baking didn't seem quite as much of a priority.

"What happened to our no-touching rule?" she asked, thinking how wonderful it felt to be in his arms again.

"I'm just giving you a little taste of what you could be experiencing right now if only you'd had your priorities straight tonight."

"Well, the night's not over yet, is it?"

"I sure hope you slept well last night, sweetheart, because you're not getting a single wink tonight."

While he still had her snugged against him, whispering a litany of truly provocative things, three faces peered around the door frame. When Ginny spied them over Cole's shoulder, the women ducked into the kitchen, giggling like high-school girls.

"I can't believe you're behaving like this!" Ginny whispered.

"Yeah, and if we don't get those cookies baked fast, you're *really* going to see some outrageous behavior. Understand?"

Ginny took him seriously—so seriously, in fact, that when Cole finally let her go into the kitchen, she discovered that the pans would hold *twenty* cookies apiece.

While Cole was busy mixing up yet another batch of cookies, Darlene whispered to Ginny.

"All those good looks, and he bakes, too?"

"He just wanted to help out," Ginny said.

"Unbelievable," Loretta said. "I mean, *really* unbelievable. I remember what he was like in high school, you know." She shook her head. "Ginny, I know what some of the people in this town have been saying about him. That he's a criminal who got away with it, a bad apple and all that. But you know, I've just decided I don't believe a word of it."

"You don't?"

"Nope. Any man who's as crazy about his wife as Cole is about you can't be bad. Trust me. I've seen plenty of bad ones to know. And if I hear any more of that kind of talk, I intend to set the record straight."

Darlene nodded. "Me, too."

It wasn't until this moment that Ginny realized the depth of the grudge the people of this town had been carrying. They'd assumed that Cole was guilty even though a jury had found him innocent, just because of what he'd been like as a teenager.

"Thanks," Ginny said. "I appreciate that."

"Hey," Loretta said. "A bunch of us are going over to the Victorian home show in Marshall in a couple of weeks. Want to come along?"

Ginny smiled, feeling a surge of pure happiness. "I'd love to."

It took another two hours, but finally the baking was done. Cole washed his hands for the last time and gave Ginny a look that said it was time to go *now*.

She felt a tingle of excitement. She knew Cole wasn't in love with her, but still he desired her in a way she'd never expected any man would.

For tonight, that would have to be enough.

The moment they said their goodbyes and walked out of Rhonda's house, Cole took Ginny by the arm.

"I want you to get into your car," he commanded, "and stay right on my tail. No slowing down and absolutely no stopping anywhere. Do you understand?"

"Well, I *was* needing some laundry soap—"

"Forget the damned laundry! You follow me home right now!"

She really shouldn't be teasing him, but she couldn't help it. "Cole? Now, you're not getting all bossy again, are you?"

He spun around, pointing a finger at her. "You bet your life

I am! Forty dozen cookies say I have a *right* to be bossy! Is that clear?"

Ginny smiled furtively. "Yes. Perfectly clear."

"Good." He yanked open her car door and she got inside. He shut it behind her and got into his car. She loved the tone of his voice, even if it was bossy. *Especially* because it was bossy.

She smiled about it all the way home. But when they passed through the gates of the ranch, suddenly it struck her exactly what they were getting ready to do, and all at once she was having a hard time breathing.

They pulled up in front of the house. Cole leaped out of his car, opened her door, took her hand and pulled her to her feet. He led her by the hand up the porch steps. The moment they stepped inside the house, he turned and pulled her against him. She wrapped her arms around his neck, desperate to feel his impatience finally unleashed into action. But instead of kissing her, he froze, staring at her.

"Cole? What's the matter?"

He opened his mouth to speak, then closed it again.

"Cole?"

"Ginny, this is...this is your first time."

"Yes. I know."

"You'll remember it for the rest of your life, whether it's good or bad—"

"Cole? What's wrong?"

"Nothing, really. It's just that—"

"Do you want to do this or not?"

"Well, yes, but—"

"But what?"

He slipped away from her and paced toward the sofa. "I feel like somehow I've pushed you into this."

"I'm the one who went on the pill. Remember?"

"Yes, I know, but still I pushed you, and—" He let out a

breath of frustration. "Look. Ginny. If you don't want to do this, you can tell me so, and I won't say another word about it. I promise."

She couldn't believe it. Was this Cole McCallum talking? Where was the cockiness, the self-assurance, the arrogant overconfidence she'd come to know so well?

Gone, at least for now. One more layer of him was peeled away, exposing the man beneath, a man who cared about her, who wanted things right for her before they could ever be right for him. And it made her want him that much more.

She walked toward him. "Cole, I want this. I want *you*. Don't you know that?"

"You say that now, but are you sure? It'll change things, Ginny. You'll feel differently afterward, and I'm not sure you're ready for that."

"Why don't you let me decide that?" She wrapped her arms around his neck. "Just kiss me."

After a moment of hesitation, he lowered his mouth to hers in a soft, gentle kiss. It was very nice, but Ginny wanted more. *Much* more.

She grabbed his shirt, pulled him down to her and kissed him. She put every ounce of feeling into it she could, using everything he'd ever taught her by example, telling him with every ounce of energy she had that she wanted him right here and right now. It was a kiss so hot and wild and intense that Cole couldn't do anything but go along for the ride.

Finally she pulled away, still gripping his shirt. She wanted to see a hot flash of desire in his eyes. She wanted to see a man on the verge of sexual explosion. She wanted to see all his hesitancy disappear so she could finally experience what she'd dreamed about most of her adult life.

Instead, he smiled. "Ginny? Are you trying to tell me something?"

She yanked on his shirt. "Yes, damn it!"

His eyes flew open wide. "Yes...*damn it?*"

"What am I going to have to do to convince you? Rip your clothes off? Rip *my* clothes off? What?"

Cole blinked with surprise. Then a smile spread slowly across his face. "Can I have both?"

Ginny dropped her forehead against his chest. "What am I going to do with you?" she moaned.

"I'll show you, sweetheart," he said gently. "Right now."

She looked at him, and there was nothing tentative about his gaze. He took her by the hand and led her into the bedroom. He swept the covers away, then pulled her down to sit beside him. He reached for the hem of her sweater, but she pushed his hands away.

"No. It's my turn."

She unfastened two of his shirt buttons. He tugged his shirttail from his jeans, then reached for her again.

A streak of boldness suddenly overtook her. She nudged his hands away, then put her hands against his shoulders and eased him down onto his back. She sensed his surprise, and she was just as surprised herself, but still she unfastened button number three, and after taking a deep, shaky breath, she spread his shirt open and kissed his chest. She wasn't at all sure it was the right thing to do, but then his eyes dropped closed and he sighed softly, giving no indication that he wanted her to stop. So she did it again with the next button, and the next, her heart beating more wildly the further down she went. He drew the sheet up in his hands, making tight fists, and she had the sudden empowering sensation that her kisses were exciting him. She unbuttoned the rest of his shirt, finishing with a kiss on his taut abdomen just above his belt buckle.

He exhaled softly. "That's really nice, sweetheart. How about the cuffs?"

Ginny unbuttoned his cuffs. He sat up and shrugged out of

the shirt, and the minute he was free of it, he grasped the hem of her sweater and pulled it off over her head. The cool air of the room hit her bare skin, but his hands were on her immediately, warming her everywhere he touched, and as soon as he unclasped her bra, his hands were there, too, stroking her with a delicious, featherlight touch.

He coaxed her to lie down, then stretched out beside her, lowering his mouth to hers in a hot, hungry kiss. She would have thought there couldn't possibly be anything more to kissing than he'd already shown her, but to her delight, he hadn't even scratched the surface yet.

After dozens of slow, deep, drugging kisses, he found the button on her jeans and undid it, then slid her zipper down. He pulled her jeans off, and she was shocked when he took her panties right along with them. Lying suddenly naked on the bed, she reached for the sheet to cover herself only to have him pull it out of her hand.

"No, you don't," he said. "I want to see all of you tonight."

So she lay there, staring at him, and she might have felt really self-conscious if she hadn't been so tuned in to Cole taking *his* jeans off. She watched as he peeled away his clothes and for the first time in her life she saw a totally naked man. In the flesh. In the most gorgeous, awe-inspiring, breathtaking flesh she'd ever seen.

Cole stretched out beside her again, his hands always moving, traveling down her body to stroke her hips, her thighs. Then she felt his hot breath against the side of her breast. He pressed a kiss there, then rose and flicked his tongue over her nipple.

Electricity shot through her. She writhed against him, but he trapped her with his hands and his body, teasing his tongue around her nipple, then doing the same to the other one. Her shock was matched only by the intense pleasure she felt, a deep pull of arousal that seemed to gather inside her, aching to be released.

"Cole?" she said, her breath coming in ragged gasps.

"Yes?"

"I want to touch you. Is that all right?"

"Is that all right?" He chuckled softly, finding it hard to imagine a scenario under which the answer to that question would be no. "Yes, sweetheart. That's all right. Just where would you like to touch me?"

She turned her head and met his eyes, giving him a heavy-lidded look that told him the location as clearly as if she'd shouted it.

She placed her hand tentatively against his hip. He guided it downward until she'd wrapped it around his shaft. She squeezed gently, exhaling as she did, and Cole clenched his teeth.

Big mistake.

Her soft, delicate fingers exploring him, stroking the length of him, the breadth of him, were making him crazy.

"It's big," she whispered.

"That's music to a man's ears," he said, a little breathlessly. "Are you sure you've never done this before?"

"Never." Her voice was so soft, so awe-filled, so serious in response to his gentle teasing, that he thanked God he was the one here with her tonight instead of some other guy who might not know just how special she was.

She got a worried look on her face. "Are you sure it'll—"

"What?"

She didn't say anything for a long time.

"Fit."

Cole smiled. He eased her onto her back. He smoothed a hand over her thigh, then moved it into the cleft between her legs. She gasped a little, but he touched his lips to hers in a calming kiss and moved his fingers deeper at the same time, delving into her wetness.

"Do you feel that, Ginny?"

"Yes," she said quietly, sounding embarrassed. "I felt that before, in the bathroom that night. Is that, you know..."

"Normal?"

"Yes."

"It's just how things are supposed to be. It's telling me you want me. And it's why fitting won't be a problem."

Then she touched him again, more boldly this time, squeezing him with those soft, soft fingers, and he knew it was time. *Now.*

He rose onto his knees, then moved between her legs. A look of apprehension came over her face.

"Don't be afraid, Ginny. I'm going to take it easy."

"I'm not afraid."

But he knew better. He could feel how nervous she was. He lowered himself to her, pressing against her without entering her, kissing her at the same time, waiting until he felt some of her tension drain away. Then he rose again and pulled her knees up. He came forward a bit and stopped, poised at her opening.

"Oh, sweetheart," he said, his breathing almost obscuring his words, "I don't want to hurt you."

"You won't."

"I might, but if I do, it'll only be for a moment."

Then he slid into her. She gasped sharply.

"Ginny? Should I stop?"

"No!" she said, clutching his shoulders. "Don't stop! Please! I want to feel it!"

He continued moving inside her, slowly at first, trying so hard to be gentle. To his surprise, after a moment he felt her hips move, and soon she'd caught his rhythm. Her eyes drifted closed, and her breathing accelerated. He thrust a little harder, a little faster, trying to hold back at the same time he wanted to fill her completely. A fire burned deep inside him, pulsing in sync with his thrusts and the rocking of her hips.

"Ah, Ginny..."

His voice was nothing but a raspy whisper. He couldn't say what he wanted to, anyway. He had no words for it. The closeness he felt to her was overpowering, the feeling of being inside her, thrusting, possessing, *needing* her so much—how could he possibly explain that to her?

She moaned softly. "Cole, I feel...like before—"

"Ginny, you're so tight, I don't know if I can—"

"Please, Cole," she breathed. "More. *Now.*"

He thrust faster, deeper, still fighting the inevitable, and a moment later he heard her sharp intake of breath. She froze, her body clamping hard around him. A flash of indescribable pleasure overtook him, and in the same moment he realized that she was there with him, clutching him, crying out, rocking hard against him, and he held her tightly as they rode the waves of pleasure together.

After the last tremors had finally subsided, he slid out of her, fell to one side and pulled her into his arms. She burrowed against him, her breathing still harsh and irregular, but as he caressed her in long, calming strokes, slowly it returned to normal. He thought maybe he ought to say something, but she lay so peacefully against him that he couldn't bear to speak.

The very idea that he'd ever thought her plain or unattractive was inconceivable to him now. Her hair shimmered in the dim light, and her eyes, with their flecks of gold, sparkled like rare jewels. She had the sweetest, softest little body he'd ever touched, round in all the right places, seemingly made just for him.

They drifted off to sleep, their legs tangled, their naked

bodies twined together. A vague thought floated through his mind that he'd never made love to a woman without having had the urge to bolt the minute it was over. But now a feeling of complete contentment overcame him, and if he had his way, he knew he would lie here with Ginny forever.

THE NEXT MORNING Ginny woke to bright sunlight filtering through the curtains. She was lying on her back with Cole's arm draped carelessly across her just beneath her breasts.

You'll feel differently afterward, and I'm not sure you're ready for that.

She quietly pushed back the covers, leaving him sleeping, then went into the bathroom and turned on the shower. For a full five minutes, she leaned against the shower wall, water streaming down her body as she fought the wonderful, terrible feeling that Cole was right.

She was in love with him.

No, she couldn't be. After all, she didn't even know what that felt like. Lust she knew. She'd felt enough of that in the past couple of months that she'd recognize it anywhere, anytime. But love? What did that feel like?

As if she wanted to stay in his arms forever. As if she wanted to lie in bed with him every night of her life. As if she didn't see him again this minute, she just might perish on the spot.

After a moment, she turned off the shower, then pulled back the curtain. Cole was waiting for her.

Naked.

He smiled. "Good morning."

Before she could step out of the shower, he stepped in. He turned on the water again, swept her into his arms, his hands and his lips everywhere at once. And before long, all her apprehension melted away.

You're a silly little fool. You'd fall in love with any man who made love to you for the first time.

She tried to make herself believe that. Tried so hard, because then it would have been easier to convince herself that when the end of their time together came, she should't give Cole another thought.

But she knew it was more than that. In the past few months, she'd seen past the face he showed to the world and had looked right into his heart, whether he'd planned on revealing it to her or not.

And that was the man she'd fallen in love with.

14

NOVEMBER on the ranch brought the final disappearance of fall colors, with brilliant orange and yellow giving way to bare tree branches and pale-brown grassland. They were preparing for winter, bringing horses in from outer pastures, stocking up on hay. Fortunately, late fall also meant cooler temperatures, which Cole welcomed.

He came home one evening to find Ginny sitting at the kitchen table, writing on a pad of paper while something bubbled on the stove. He'd had a hard day hauling hay, and all he could think about right now was getting a shower, having dinner and dragging Ginny to bed.

She turned around with a bright smile. "How would you like to go camping?"

Cole stopped dead in his tracks. Camping? He couldn't think of anything he'd like to do *less*.

"We could go this weekend. Stay Friday and Saturday nights. We could camp and fish and have cookouts and watch the sunset and all that other outdoor stuff. Doesn't that sound like fun?"

Actually, no. It sounded like hell on earth. "Come on, Ginny. I spend all day every day outdoors. Indoors the rest of the time suits me just fine."

"But I've never been camping before. I really want to go. I've made a list right here of everything we'll need."

"Where'd you get such an idea?"

"I saw the camping gear down at the barn, and Murphy said it'd be okay if we used it."

Murphy. He should have known. Was that man destined to be a thorn in his side for the rest of his life? Ginny was looking at him with that sweet little expression of hope, the one that said he would feel like a heel if he said no.

"So?" Ginny said. "Do you want to go?"

"Do you have any idea how cold the nights are this time of year?"

"We'll make a fire. And sleep in a tent. Murphy says the sleeping bags will keep us warm even in subzero temperatures."

"Friday *and* Saturday night?" he asked.

"Yeah." She eased next to him, wrapped her arms around his neck and kissed him.

"Does the tent have soundproof walls?"

Ginny drew back. "Do they have those on tents?"

"Do you think we'll need them?"

"We'll be way out in the middle of nowhere." She grinned. "Maybe."

"Then I'll go."

ON FRIDAY it was nearly dark by the time they arrived at the lake. They found a secluded clearing, set up the tent and built a fire. They roasted some hot dogs, then sat on a blanket by the fire to eat.

"This is *so* good," Ginny said, starting on her second hot dog. "I never knew something could taste so wonderful cooked over a fire. Oh! And I brought the stuff for s'mores. I've never had those before, but I can't imagine not liking them. With graham crackers, marshmallows and chocolate they can't help but be good, right?"

She was having such a wonderful time that pretty soon

Cole caught her enthusiasm and decided a little trek into the wilderness hadn't been such a bad idea, after all.

After they ate, Cole threw another log on the fire, and Ginny snuggled close to him. She'd changed so much over these past few weeks, going from naive virgin to eager lover, and he couldn't get enough of her. At the same time he knew that it was going to come to an end in a few weeks and they'd be going their separate ways. He had a life to pursue, and so did she. But was there any reason they couldn't enjoy their time together until then?

"Time for bed," Cole said.

"Bed? It's only eight-thirty!"

"Is there something you'd rather do?"

Ginny smiled. "Can't think of a thing."

They picked up things around the campsite, then went into the tent. Cole pulled the tent flap down and zipped it, then turned to Ginny.

"Okay, sweetheart," he said. "Time to get naked."

"Are you kidding? It's fifty degrees in here!"

"Ah, but you should have thought of that when you invited me on a camping trip. Did you think I'd actually let you stay bundled up like Nanook of the North?" He grinned. "Off with it."

Ginny looked a little shy, but to her credit, she rose to the challenge. Off came her coat. Then her boots. She pulled her sweatshirt over her head, then dropped her jeans to the floor of the tent.

"Cole," she said. "You're staring at me."

"Did you think I wouldn't?"

"I'm freezing!"

He dropped his gaze a bit. "I can tell."

Ginny glared at him. "You're downright lecherous."

"Never said I wasn't."

She quickly removed her bra and panties, then dived into

the double sleeping bag, yanking it over her. As Cole started taking off his clothes, she gave him a lecherous grin of her own.

Moments later he was bundled up inside the sleeping bag with her. To his surprise, she pushed him onto his back and kissed him, a long, lingering kiss with her breasts pressed firmly to his chest. He'd gotten a little worked up watching her subzero striptease, and the feel of her warm, naked body next to his was turning up the heat even more. She continued to kiss him, her hand roaming across his chest, his abdomen. Then she slipped her hand lower and caressed him in the most intimate way possible, squeezing gently, rubbing slowly up and down, sending him halfway to heaven in a matter of seconds.

He couldn't believe this was the same woman who hadn't experienced so much as a kiss only a few short months ago. He also couldn't believe he was on the verge of losing it and she'd barely even touched him.

"Whoa," he said, pulling his lips away from hers and taking her hand in his.

"What?"

"I'm getting a little too excited here, sweetheart."

"That's a bad thing?"

He laughed. "No, it's not a *bad* thing—"

"Then hush."

Cole was in awe of what this woman could do to him with a single word, a single touch. She'd become a willing pupil who didn't think twice about teaching the teacher a thing or two, and he loved every minute of it. She began touching him again, and all she wanted him to do was lie back and let it happen. But he had no intention of letting things go at that.

He rose and eased her onto her back. She reached for him, urging him to move on top of her, but instead he pressed her thighs apart and moved between them, rubbing his hands upward in slow circles toward the apex of her thighs. He eased his fingers into her cleft, and she closed her eyes and sighed softly. She felt so hot and wet that he could have entered her and she would have been ready for him, but he had other things in mind. He moved his hand upward, found the place she was the most sensitive and lingered there, touching her, rubbing her...*kissing* her.

Her eyes sprang open. "Cole—"

She squirmed against him. He held her hips steady. "Relax, sweetheart," he whispered, dropping a gentle kiss just below her navel. "It's okay. Really. It's perfectly normal, I promise you."

"I know," she said breathlessly, every muscle in her body suddenly tense. "I—I was at the library the other day, and there was this book...."

He touched her with his tongue, swirling it enticingly.

"I—I learned a few things about stuff like this, but—"

He stroked her with his tongue.

"I never thought you'd actually—"

He closed his mouth over her and sucked gently. Her whole body stiffened.

"Good *heavens!*"

Her voice was filled with wonder, and Cole couldn't help smiling. She seemed to be ready to bolt and dying for him to continue all at the same time, putting her in a state of such heightened awareness he could almost hear her body hum. The fact that she'd been doing a little self-study pleased him to no end. And he wanted to please her to no end.

He continued to tease his tongue over her, caressing her thighs at the same time. Her hands fluttered against his shoulders as if she were unsure where to put them, but then slowly he felt her fingers tighten. Her accelerated breathing became harsh and needy. Instead of shifting uneasily back and forth, she began to move subtly with his rhythm, arching her hips to meet him. She moaned softly, rolling her head in a semicircle, her fingernails digging into his shoulders.

"Cole..."

He increased the pressure, clasping her thighs in his hands, loving the hot, silky sound of her voice as she spoke his name.

"Cole, no...not yet..."

He continued.

"No...please..."

He had no intention of stopping.

"Cole!"

Before he knew what was happening, she'd squirmed away from him, sat up suddenly and pushed him onto *his* back. She put her leg over his thighs to sit astride him. And it shocked the hell out of him.

She stared at him, her hands against his shoulders. "I want you inside me," she said, her breath coming so hard she was barely able to speak. "We have to do it together."

He must have still looked shocked, because she gave him a smile and said, "It's okay, Cole. It's perfectly normal. I promise you."

He laughed, thrilled that his repressed little virgin was no longer repressed in the least. "This book you read was in the *Coldwater* Public Library?"

"Yes. Can you believe it?"

"Just for the record, I'll take you to the library anytime you want to go."

She shifted slightly, then lowered herself slowly, slowly onto him. He put his hands on her hips and pulled her down until he was deep inside her. She began to move, sliding up and down on his shaft, easing into a slow, seductive rhythm that took his breath away.

"Yeah, sweetheart," he murmured. "Just like that."

He took her breasts in his hands, squeezing them gently, then stroked his thumbs across her nipples. They felt like hard little pebbles. That told him it was probably cold in the tent, but what Ginny was doing to him was making him feel hot all the way to the bone. She ran her hands down his arms to his shoulders and back up again, still moving, always moving, giving him pleasure at the same time she was seeking her own.

"Cole..."

Her voice was barely above a whisper, but he heard an undercurrent of pure excitement. Her eyes were squeezed closed, her cheeks flushed pink, her windblown hair framing her head like a tangled halo. He clamped his hands onto her hips and urged her harder, faster, losing himself in the mindless pleasure of their bodies moving as if they'd been born to make love together. Until now, it hadn't much mattered whom he was with because it had been about pure sexual release and nothing else. So why with Ginny did it feel like so much more?

Her breathing became deep and raspy, her movements urgent, and soon he could tell her climax was only moments away. Heat pooled in his groin, stoked by the sound of her voice, the feel of her body moving on top of his. Then all at once she cried out his name, driving down on him again, her body convulsing, and that's all it took to push him over the edge with her.

He pulled her down and tightened his arms around her, her breasts crushed against his chest, groaning at the sudden, indescribable sensation that had exploded inside him. She shuddered in his arms, moaning softly, which only added fuel to his fire and made his climax seem to go on forever.

She lay on top of him for a long time afterward, his arms encircling her. They were still joined together, her cheek against his shoulder. Finally she fell to one side, and he pulled her into his arms.

"I can't believe I just did that," she said. "I mean, I saw it in the book, but—"

"How many pages were in that book?"

"I don't know. Maybe two hundred."

"Did you read it all?"

"Not yet. I was too chicken to check it out."

"How far did you get?"

"Page one hundred and forty."

"Are you planning on finishing it?"

"Oh, yes."

"Will you be demonstrating what's in those last sixty pages?"

Ginny smiled. "Only if you want me to."

"Oh, I want you to, sweetheart. Believe me."

She snuggled next to him, and he pulled the sleeping bag around them, wrapping them in a cocoon of warmth. Her eyes slowly drifted closed. He stared at her in awe, still unable to believe just how beautiful she was and how blind he must have been not to see that. It was beauty unlike any he'd ever expected to find in a woman—naïveté and innocence wrapped in joy and enthusiasm and pure goodness, and suddenly sex didn't seem like just sex anymore, but a connection he'd never felt with anyone else.

It's because you've been around her longer than you've ever been around a woman before. Of course you'd start to feel something. It's called friendship. You're friends. That's all. Friends who have lots of hot sex, but friends just the same. And soon even that will be over.

They had fewer than two weeks together left. He felt a rush of regret, then chased the feeling away, focusing instead on the moment at hand, because when it came right down to it, that was the only thing that was real. He'd known from the start, just as Ginny had, that this would be coming to an end.

Because nothing, no matter how good it was, could possibly last forever.

15

THE NEXT DAY, Ginny was still reeling from her night of love-making with Cole, blushing when she thought about the things they'd done, and for just a moment when she woke, she almost couldn't look at him. She was afraid that in the light of day he would think she was some kind of sex-crazed hussy to allow such things, to *do* such things. But then he smiled at her, a broad, dazzling smile that told her not only had he liked what they'd done together last night, he would be willing to do it again anytime she said the word.

After a leisurely breakfast, he taught her the basics of fishing, a sport she decided she could do without. Well, holding the pole was okay, and watching the little red-and-white bobber thing, and turning the little knob to pull a fish to shore, but baiting the hook and taking the fish off the hook were tasks she left to Cole. In the end it was all pretty pointless anyway, since she felt sorry for every fish they caught and insisted he throw them all back. Nevertheless she got to sit with Cole beside that lake and talk to him when the fish weren't biting, which was most of the time. Suddenly fishing didn't seem so bad, after all.

They relaxed all afternoon, taking a walk along a two-mile nature trail they found. They spent a surprising amount of time at the lakeshore, skipping rocks off the water. Ginny thoroughly enjoyed herself, refusing to think about the fact that their time together would be over before she knew it.

Cole seemed to grow quieter as the day wore on, and when

evening came and dinner was over, there were long moments when he did nothing but pull her close to him and stare into the fire. And when they finally slipped into their tent together, he drew her into his arms without a word and made love to her with a sweet intensity that took her breath away.

Afterward they lay together, tucked inside the sleeping bag, Ginny's head resting on Cole's shoulder.

"So," Ginny said softly. "I guess you'll be selling the ranch pretty soon."

Cole sighed. That was the last thing he wanted to talk about right now. "Yeah. I guess I will."

"And that means the horses, too?"

"Yeah, the horses, too."

"Can I buy Sunday from you?"

"What?"

"I was thinking maybe I could find a stable in Austin and keep her there. I know I'll miss riding, and she's such a sweet horse—"

"Ginny, if you want her, she's yours. Saddle, bridle, whatever you want. You can have one of the horse trailers, too. How would that be?"

"That'd be wonderful. Thank you."

She acted as if it was a big favor he was doing her, but to him it seemed like such a small thing after all they'd been through together. There was the twenty-five thousand, but that was money. An impersonal pile of cash. He'd already been thinking about what it was going to be like to hand her that check, and it made him feel very uneasy.

"So what are you planning to do when you get back to Dallas?" she asked. "Invest in that apartment complex?"

"Probably. Among other things."

"I guess you're pretty good at making money."

"Yeah, I guess I am."

"You know, you've been telling me lately that I need to

start looking at myself differently so I can be something more." She rose on her elbows and stared at him. "How about you, Cole? When are you going to start looking at yourself differently so you can have more out of life?"

"I've already had it all, Ginny. I lost it, but it wasn't my fault. And the minute I get some seed money back in my hands, I'm going to—"

"Money? Do you think that's what I'm talking about? Don't define yourself that way, Cole. There's more to life than that."

"Maybe, but money makes life a whole lot easier. Believe me. If you have enough of it, nobody can touch you."

"Maybe it's time you let somebody touch you."

He had the sudden uncanny sense that Ginny could see right inside him, and he didn't like the feeling. He gave her a cocky smile.

"Sure, sweetheart. Touch me all you want to."

Ginny sat up suddenly. "Stop it, Cole."

"What's the matter? I was only joking."

"Well, cut it out."

He sat up beside her. "I don't get it. What's wrong?"

"Anytime I mention something you don't want to talk about, you find a way to squirm out of it."

"No, I don't."

"Don't believe me? Then tell me about your grandmother. Why did you visit her only four times in ten years?"

Cole blinked with surprise. "Who told you that?"

"Murphy."

"That figures," he said, lying down again.

"Answer the question."

He started to tell her once again that it was none of her business, but suddenly his heart was beating rapidly, and he had a dry, harsh feeling in his throat. He swallowed hard, but the feeling remained.

"I don't know," he said finally.

"Did you love her?"

"Yes, of course I did."

"Then why didn't you come back to see her more often?"

She was going to think he was stonewalling again, but the truth was he honestly didn't know.

"Cole, there must be some reason—"

"I told you. I don't know."

"Murphy says it was nothing but ingratitude."

"You need to stop talking to Murphy."

"I think you were afraid to go see her."

"Afraid? Hardly. Murphy didn't intimidate me any more then than he does now."

"Murphy had nothing to do with it."

Cole suddenly felt hot, even though the temperature in the tent couldn't possibly have been more than fifty-five degrees. "What do you think, then?" he asked with a hollow laugh. "That I was afraid of my grandmother?"

"Yes. In a way I think you were."

"That's crazy."

Ginny slipped her hand over his. "After your father and your mother were gone, I think you were afraid that nobody could possibly love you. You didn't believe that somebody would ever be there for you tomorrow just like they were there for you today. So no matter how much your grandmother showed you she loved you, you were always waiting for the other shoe to fall."

Cole stared at the ceiling of the tent, his heart racing. All at once he felt now as he'd felt then, that all-encompassing pain and disbelief that had swept over him when he'd been told that his father—the only parent he had left—had been thrown in jail, leaving him with nobody. And then his grandmother had stepped in, showering him with more love and affection than he'd ever known. But every bit of experience he'd had told him anything that wonderful couldn't possibly be real, and if by some chance it was, it couldn't possibly last.

"So you were afraid to come back," Ginny said. "Afraid if you came to see her again, that other shoe would fall. You'd find out she had abandoned you, just as everybody else in your life had."

"My grandmother never would have done that."

"Logically you knew that, but logic isn't always what drives us, is it? And actually, in a way she did abandon you. She died. Whether it was her fault or not, one day she just wasn't there for you anymore."

Cole was suddenly caught in a whirlwind of memories. His grandmother in her kitchen, feeding him, talking to him, pretending whatever reprimand he'd gotten at school that day was water under the bridge. And then that awful day years later when Murphy had called to tell him she'd had a stroke. He remembered driving ninety miles an hour on I-20, trying to get to the hospital, only to find her dead by the time he got there. And there was Murphy, staring at him accusingly, as though somehow it had been his fault.

After the funeral came the will. He hadn't understood a bit of that, why his grandmother had done what she'd done, and his confusion had made him so defensive that when he finally left town, he and Murphy had been only one angry remark away from an all-out brawl.

He remembered everything that had happened. What he'd hidden away was how he'd *felt* about it, that gut-wrenching sensation of being alone in the world again. Somehow he'd shut all that out, but here it was again, and it just about tore him apart.

"I was seven years old when my mother left," he told Ginny, feeling as if he were in a daze, as if somebody's else's words were coming out of his mouth. "I got home from school one day and nobody was there. I sat there crying for two hours until my father got home. He searched their bedroom, realized she was gone, then came into the kitchen and told me to stop crying, that we were better off without her. Then he pulled a bottle of whiskey out of the cabinet, got drunk and passed out. I never saw my mother again."

He glanced at Ginny and saw tears in her eyes. He didn't want that. He didn't want sympathy. He just wanted...

Hell, he didn't know what he wanted. He pulled Ginny into his arms. He had the most irrational feeling that as long as he held her, the pain might go away. She rested her palm against his chest under the blankets, moving her thumb back and forth in calm, soothing strokes.

"My grandmother," he whispered. "I never told her I loved her."

"It doesn't matter," Ginny said. "I have a feeling she always knew."

Cole rose on one elbow and stared at Ginny, holding on to a tiny shred of hope that maybe she was right. He slipped his hand behind her neck, tangling his fingers in her hair, then drew her close for a long, lingering kiss.

He felt his body stir, and he couldn't believe that so soon after making love he was ready to do it again. As he took Ginny into his arms, he had loose, fragmented thoughts of how warm she felt against him, how soft and enticing she was and how he'd come to depend on her so much. And somewhere in the deep recesses of his mind he saw a dim light, a faint beacon calling him to a place he'd never been before.

Tell her. Tell her you love her.

The words swirled around inside his head, floating like an apparition but never quite taking hold. He'd felt bits and pieces of them for a long time, always shoving them to the back of his mind, but still they were there—in every stolen glance, in every moment of silent togetherness, in every satisfied sigh in the dark.

He'd told himself for a long time that his relationship with Ginny was just sex, that in the end it was no more permanent than it had been with any other woman he'd held in his arms. But later as they lay together, totally exhausted and on the very edge of sleep, the words came to him again.

Tell her you love her.

No. It was just an illusion. A dream. He was dreaming about a forever kind of love like a man dying of thirst dreams of water. He wants it so desperately that when he sees a mirage in the distance, he crawls toward it, filled with hope, only to have those hopes shatter when he finally reaches it and realizes it was never real in the first place. And Cole knew he'd rather die of thirst than risk touching that mirage only to pull his hand back to find nothing but sand slipping through his fingers.

THE NEXT MORNING they headed back to the ranch. Cole was quiet all the way home, as he had been all morning, and Ginny knew he was thinking about last night. She'd made him face some things he hadn't wanted to, and she wasn't completely sure he was happy about it.

Maybe she'd pushed him too hard, but it was so easy to see how much he was hurting and how badly he needed to talk about it. If she had known he was going to give her the cold shoulder, though, she wasn't sure she would have said anything, no matter how much he needed to talk. Maybe it was selfish, but she wanted nothing to get in the way of them enjoying every minute of the time they had left together.

In the tent last night, she'd asked him about Sunday because she really did want the horse, but deep down she'd also wanted to make absolutely sure his plans to sell the ranch still stood. They did. He'd made it clear from the beginning they'd be splitting up in six months. She'd even signed a contract that said so. So why was she despondent now?

Because you love him.

She had to get that out of her mind. She might be in love with him, but he'd made it clear she was nothing more than a stopover for him. He would be moving on again. She felt a little choked up at the thought of that, then chastised herself. What had she expected, anyway? That he would fall madly in love with her and want to be with her forever?

After they arrived home and he still seemed withdrawn, Ginny wondered if she should say something to him—ask him what was wrong, apologize for coming on so strong last night—*something*. But in the end she said nothing, and by the time they sat down that afternoon to watch football, he seemed to have come back to life a little bit, and she decided he needed a little time to let it all soak in.

He got up during halftime, leaving Ginny sitting on the sofa, and a minute later she heard him call to her from the bedroom. She went to the doorway to find him sitting on the bed, his back to her.

"Yes?"

"Come over here."

She walked to the bed.

"Sit down."

His voice was cold. Commanding. She sat down beside him, and for the first time she realized he was holding something.

Her pill case.

For a moment, Ginny couldn't breathe. It had been here all weekend. She'd forgotten to take it with her.

"According to this," Cole said, "you've missed two days. Is that right?"

"I—I guess I have," she murmured. She swallowed hard. "What if—"

"No," Cole said. "Don't even think it."

"It's...possible."

Cole let out a harsh breath, then tossed the pills on the nightstand. "I can't believe you forgot!"

"I'm sorry," she murmured.

"Sorry? You're sorry? Is that all you can say?"

Ginny flinched, tears coming to her eyes.

"A week and a half away," he muttered. "A week and a half..."

A week and a half. He was talking about the rest of their time together as if he was on the verge of being released from prison, only to be looking at the possibility of getting stuck with a life sentence.

He stood up and strode to the dresser, then turned back, a strange glint in his eyes. "Are you sure you just forgot?"

Ginny blinked. "What are you saying?"

"You know what I'm saying."

When it finally dawned on her what he meant, she was so startled that for a moment she couldn't speak.

"I would *never*—" She took a deep, angry breath. "You *know* I would never do that to you!"

"Do I? Twenty-five thousand dollars is one thing, Ginny. Half of this ranch is another thing entirely."

Ginny was so flabbergasted she barely knew what to say. "You think I'm trying to *trap* you into staying married?"

He looked at her coldly. "You wouldn't be the first one to try it."

How could he say these things to her? How? After everything they'd meant to each other?

Or maybe she'd just imagined that. His face was so cold and dark she felt as if she were looking at a stranger.

"I—I can't believe you're saying these things."

"And I can't believe I bought all that talk about your being so afraid of getting pregnant. If you'd been so afraid, Ginny, you wouldn't have forgotten."

"But I *did* forget! They were here in the bedroom because I took them every evening when I went to bed so I *wouldn't* forget, but when I was getting ready to go camping, all my other stuff was in the bathroom, and...and I just forgot!"

"And you're telling me that for two days you didn't even think about it?"

She hadn't. Not once. She'd been having such a wonderful time, in an atmosphere so different from home, that she just hadn't remembered until the moment she looked down and saw him holding the pills.

"Maybe you didn't read the fine print in our prenuptial agreement. Under no circumstances are you entitled to one dime from the proceeds of the sale of this ranch."

She was horrified. "Is that what you think? That I want your money?"

"Sure you do. Twenty-five thousand dollars at the very least."

"You can keep your twenty-five thousand dollars!"

"Oh, I can? Well, if you don't want that, then what *do* you want?"

He glared at her, challenging her, daring her to spell out her real motives. He had absolutely no idea what she was thinking, what she'd been thinking for weeks now, what she'd been dying to tell him but just hadn't been able to bring herself to do it.

"You, Cole. That's what I want."

The truth. She whispered it so softly that the words were barely audible. She hadn't completely crystallized it in her mind until this very moment, until the prospect of tomorrow without him became so painfully real.

"It's all I've wanted for the longest time. Just you."

His face remained impassive. "Sorry, sweetheart. I'm not buying that. The average woman has her eyes on my wallet from day one and never lets it out of her sight."

"That's because the average woman isn't in love with you."

The air between them became deathly still. For the count of three, neither of them spoke, and just for a moment, his expression betrayed him. She saw a light in his eyes, an opening, a way to reach inside him. But just as quickly his expression hardened again, his face shrouded in cynicism.

"So you're in love with me," he said with a small, humorless laugh. "I guess you haven't been paying attention, have you? We've been stuck together in this one-horse town for so long that you've forgotten who I really am. I'm the guy who talked you into marriage for his own financial gain. I'm the guy most people think just might be guilty of arson. I'm the guy who thinks nothing of having a different woman in his bed every night. Now, maybe I've put all that aside for a while, but in the long run, it's who I am, and if you're smart, you'll *never* forget that."

Ginny tried hard not to cry, but tears welled in her eyes. She felt dizzy, as if she couldn't get enough air to breathe, as if the bedroom were rocking back and forth. This wasn't the Cole she knew. Why was he acting like this? *Why?* They'd been so close, and now...

That was it.

All at once she remembered everything he'd said last night in the tent, and the answer came to her in a rush of understanding.

For weeks now, as he'd grown closer and closer to her, sharing things with her he'd never shared with anyone else, making love with her, knowing she cared about him...

He'd been waiting for the other shoe to fall.

He'd trusted her. For one of the few times in his life, he'd given a piece of his heart away, and right now he was absolutely certain she'd taken advantage of that. Even if she hadn't this time, it was inevitable, so he figured he might as well end it now. And in the event she actually was so misguided to think she might be in love with him, he'd reminded her of what a rotten person he was so there was no way she could ever have that misconception again.

"But don't worry," Cole added. "If you're pregnant, I'll take legal responsibility. You'll have all the financial support you need."

"Oh," she murmured. "So we're back to money again?"

"It's what makes the world go around."

"Tell me, Cole. If your father had given you money, would that have been enough?"

Cole's eyes grew cold and bitter. He turned and headed for the bedroom door.

"Cole?"

He turned back.

"If you were looking for an excuse to drive me away, this one was as good as any, wasn't it?"

"It's over, Ginny. In a week and a half, we'll be divorced. You'll go your way, and I'll go mine. And that'll be that."

16

TWO HOURS LATER, Ginny sat at Rhonda's kitchen table, tissues close at hand. Two suitcases sat next to the refrigerator. They contained everything she'd been able to stuff inside them on short notice.

After Cole had left the house, she'd felt so lost and alone she called Rhonda, who had offered to let her stay with her as long as she needed to. Ginny was thankful for that, because she knew she couldn't look at the accusation in Cole's eyes anymore. As misguided as he was, still he believed she'd betrayed him, and nothing would ever change his mind.

She'd told Rhonda everything, from the night at the Lone Wolf to her encounter with Cole in the bedroom today and everything in between.

"Please don't say anything about this to anyone else," she begged Rhonda once the story was told. "Murphy doesn't want anyone to know about the will, and—and I don't want anyone to know about it, either."

"You know you can trust me, Ginny. I won't say anything to anyone. I swear I won't."

Ginny put her hand to her abdomen. Rhonda had called a clinic to find out how far along she had to be before a pregnancy test would be accurate, and they told her to come in in a week to ten days. The odds were probably against it, but what if it really were true? She already knew how Cole felt about it. He'd give her money for support. Nothing more. But he'd never promised himself. Not in any way. Not from the first time she'd made this deal with him until this very minute. And if she'd ever thought otherwise, she'd been sadly mistaken.

"Cole *will* take responsibility, won't he?" Rhonda asked.

"Oh, yeah. No problem. He said he'd give me all the money I need."

Ginny buried her face in her hands and the tears came again. Rhonda patted her arm. "I'm so sorry, sweetie."

There was one part of her story she'd left out, though it appeared Rhonda had already guessed the essence of it anyway—the part where she'd told Cole she loved him.

Why had she done that? Why? Now, for the rest of her life, she would look back on the moment and feel humiliated, always seeing that look in his eyes that said she was some kind of deluded little fool.

She wanted so desperately to make him believe she hadn't betrayed him, but she knew how hopeless that would be. He'd grown up in a situation where everyone he'd ever loved turned their backs on him. By the time he found his grandmother, he was so emotionally fragile he couldn't even tell her he loved her. And now ten more years had hardened him into a man nobody could touch.

Not even Ginny.

WHEN COLE returned to the house three hours later, Ginny was gone.

He came into the kitchen. Total silence, except for the wall clock ticking. He saw a note on the table.

I'll be at Rhonda's. Ginny.

He supposed she'd done that so he wouldn't worry about her.

He tossed the note on the table and sank into a kitchen chair. He'd been so angry when he left the house he'd wanted desperately to hit something. Instead he'd taken his anger out on the accelerator of his car, and right now he considered himself lucky he hadn't wrapped his car around a tree.

But, no, he'd managed to get home in one piece. As if anyone gave a damn.

He sat in the kitchen for several minutes, the only sound that infernal clock ticking. When he couldn't stand it any longer, he got up, pulled it off the wall, yanked the battery out of it and tossed both the battery and the clock in the trash can. Then he returned to the table and wished he'd left it ticking.

The silence was worse.

She told me she loved me.

Love. The most meaningless word in the English language. Of course she would tell him that—she wanted his money. Any woman would when the payoff was that big. And what was a little pregnancy, too, compared to that kind of loot?

It had been a mirage, after all. A bone-dry handful of sand.

He didn't feel angry anymore. He just felt numb. He knew this kitchen had once been filled with warmth and laughter, but for the life of him, he couldn't feel it now. He tried to remember what it had been like to kiss Ginny, to hear her voice, to feel her body beneath his, to hear her crying out with pleasure, but it was as if his entire nervous system had shut down, leaving him feeling...nothing.

It was just as well, because the woman he'd felt something for had tried to use him, maybe even worse than he'd used her. He laughed a little at that, a harsh, hollow laugh that sounded empty to his ears.

Somehow he would get through this next week and a half. Then he would put the ranch on the market, hit I-20 and head to Dallas. With luck he would never have to set foot in Coldwater, Texas, again.

IT TOOK Murphy two days to realize something was up.

Cole showed up at the barn one morning and was met with the old man's stony stare.

"Where's Ginny?"

Cole heaved a bale of hay into the breezeway of the barn, wishing Murphy would go away and leave him alone. That's all he wanted. Just to be left alone.

"She's at work, I imagine."

"No. I mean she hasn't been around the barn in a few days, and come to think of it, I haven't seen her car, either."

Cole clipped the bale open with a pair of wire cutters and tossed some in a hayrack in one of the stalls. "She's staying with a friend for a little while."

Murphy took a threatening step forward. "What did you do to her?"

Cole spun around. "What did I do to her? What do you mean, what did I *do* to her? She's staying with a friend. What's so hard to understand about that?"

He turned away and took a deep, silent breath, knowing he'd spoken too loudly and too angrily. But the old man shouldn't be sticking his nose where it didn't belong.

"There's obviously more to it than that," Murphy said.

"Even if there is, it's none of your business."

"Yeah, I think it is my business. I know how you've been using Ginny, and why. She's so young, and naive—"

"She knew the score going in."

"Oh, yeah. I'm sure you made a rock-solid argument with her. You bought yourself a wife for twenty-five thousand dollars. I don't know all the details, but I'm betting the deal was pretty cold. You even got her to sign a contract, didn't you?"

Cole looked away.

"That's what I thought."

"I've never lied to Ginny. Never."

"Not in so many words, you haven't. But I've seen the two of you together down at the barn lately. I can tell—"

"Stop it, Murphy."

"—that there's something between you. And the fact that you're acting as if there isn't—"

"There's nothing between Ginny and me! I don't want anything to do with her!"

"Good God!" Murphy shouted. "Some men wait their whole lives for a woman to look at them the way she looks at you! Are you blind?"

Cole recoiled, Murphy's words striking him like a hammer blow. All the sudden images of Ginny's face floated through his mind, that sweet, sweet face that looked at him as no other woman ever had before. With kindness. With compassion.

With love, if there was such a thing.

"I can't settle down," Cole said, suddenly a little shaky. "I don't even want to try. I've got business in Dallas—"

"Oh, yeah. It's always the next deal, isn't it? That's the most important thing to you." Murphy spat into the dust. "You're just like your father. And sooner or later—"

Cole took a double fistful of Murphy's shirt and shoved him against a stall door. "Don't you *ever* say that to me again. I'm *nothing* like my father!"

Murphy glared at him. "He always had a temper, too. Couldn't control it any better than you can."

Cole slowly released his hold on Murphy's shirt and backed away, trembling with anger.

Murphy stared at Cole long and hard. "The only reason I've played along with this charade so far is because Edna wanted me to, no matter what, as long as you technically fulfilled the terms of the will. But Ginny's gone now. That means you're not living together anymore. By all rights I can shut this deal down anytime I want to. Now, you could take me to court, but once it comes out how you manipulated the situation—"

"Then why don't you do it? Just do it! Pull the plug on this whole deal. Keep the ranch yourself, sell it, *burn* it. I just don't give a damn. But don't you *dare* bring up Ginny's name to me again!"

Murphy met his angry gaze head-on. "I don't know exactly what you did to that girl, but I'm glad she had the smarts to leave. She deserves somebody a whole lot better than you. And I hope to hell she finds him."

Murphy turned and stalked out of the barn, leaving Cole standing there breathing hay dust and hating him more with every breath he took.

Because the old man was right.

LATE THAT NIGHT, Cole sat at the kitchen table, opening the envelope that contained his and Ginny's marriage license. He looked at the stamp on it from the Clark County Courthouse, and the signatures of the proprietors of Cupid's Little Chapel of Love. Then there was Ginny's signature—tiny, feminine and reserved. A signature that mirrored her personality exactly.

He tossed it aside and picked up their contract. Pages and pages of legalese he'd paid an attorney to draw up that even he didn't completely understand. It had been intended as intimidation as much as anything else. He'd wanted to insure that whatever woman he married wouldn't step out of line and that he had complete control of the situation.

Suddenly he had no control of the situation at all.

Pregnancy. Ginny might be pregnant. Which meant he would be a father.

That scared him. Scared him more than anything in his life ever had. Just the word conjured up images he'd spent his whole life trying to forget.

How in the *hell* could she have forgotten those pills?

If she'd been as afraid of getting pregnant as she said she was, she couldn't have. Which meant she'd forgotten on purpose.

But had she really?

Stop it. She's the one who betrayed you, not the other way around. No way could she have just forgotten.

But no matter how many times he repeated that to himself, no matter how many times he tried to make himself believe it, he couldn't. A slow, nagging feeling ate away at him until he couldn't stand it any longer.

Ginny had never meant to forget those pills.

Suddenly he felt nauseated, as if he truly was going to be sick, and he had the oddest burning sensation behind his eyes.

Tears.

What was the matter with him? He ground the heels of his hands into his eyes, desperate to rub them away.

The phone rang.

He yanked up the receiver. "Hello?"

"Hey, McCallum. Have I got some news for you."

Cole took a deep, silent breath. Dave Fletcher. Not now. He didn't want to talk to this guy right now.

"You're not going to believe this. The neighborhood that apartment complex is sitting in has just been declared a historical preservation area. I'd say the value just shot up by twenty percent, and we're holding an option to buy at fifty percent of the old market value. So what do you think about that, partner?"

Cole sat there, Fletcher's words passing right through him as if he hadn't even heard them. There had been a time when words like that would have set him on fire. Now they were nothing but white noise.

"McCallum? Are you there?"

"Yeah. I'm here."

"We're going to make a killing on this deal. A *killing*."

Cole's mind felt dark and blurry. He played back the terrible words he'd spoken to Ginny like some kind of surreal nightmare.

How could he have accused her of such a thing? She was the one person on this earth who loved him, the one person who understood him as nobody else did. They were the same, he and Ginny. They'd lived with the same kind of pain coming from the same kind of place—the feeling of being alone in the world with nobody to give a damn if you lived or died. Of trying to meet the expectations of the rest of the world and not quite measuring up. Ginny had cowered because of it, while he'd stood up and shouted at the top of his lungs that he just didn't give a damn. Either way, though, the result was the same, and when he looked at her, he saw himself reflected back, and in her eyes was an understanding he'd never expected to see in another human being.

How could he have known that she was the one person on this earth who could unlock his heart and crawl right inside it?

It's all I've wanted for the longest time, Cole. Just you.

He cradled the phone against his shoulder and rubbed his temples with his fingertips, staring at the divorce papers. Right now, she was his wife. In a few days, when he filed the forms, all that would be over with.

Fletcher was rattling on about painting contractors and landscape architects, but Cole let his words go in one ear and out the other. All he could think about was how much he loved Ginny, a love that seemed to grow with every breath he took. Why hadn't he seen it before?

For the past six months he'd been so consumed with making that next buck he'd ignored the one thing that would make him happy for the rest of his life, money or not. But how would he ever convince her nothing in this world mattered to him more than she did?

He glanced at the divorce papers. He froze for a moment, then picked them up, staring at the dates. All at once he knew what he had to do. It might take him a few days, but surely he could get it done in time, and then—

"McCallum! Hey! Are you there?"

"Yeah. I'm here."

"So how's it looking?"

"How's what looking?"

"Your cash flow! Man, aren't you listening? We've got a one-year option, so you have some time. But give me a projected date on the windfall you're expecting."

"Sorry, Fletcher. I've decided against this one."

"*What?*"

"I'm backing out."

"Are you nuts? This one is going to be a gold mine!"

"With those kinds of numbers on the project, you won't have any trouble finding another partner."

"Yeah, but you're the guy I want."

"Sorry. You'll have to do without me on this one."

He heard Fletcher sigh with disgust. "McCallum, I don't think you know what you're doing."

Cole folded the divorce papers and put them into the envelope. "Actually, for the first time in my life, I think I do."

17

SEVERAL DAYS later, Ginny sat with Rhonda at her kitchen table, fingering the piece of paper she held. On it was the phone number of the clinic where she'd had her pregnancy test done earlier that day.

It was after four o'clock. They would have the results. In only a few minutes, she would know if she was pregnant. If she wasn't, she would never see Cole again. If she was, she would see his checks for years to come. Either prospect was enough to make tears come to her eyes.

"It's now or never, sweetie," Rhonda said.

Ginny picked up the telephone.

Suddenly she heard a knock on Rhonda's front door. Rhonda got up to open it. Ginny heard a commotion in the living room, then turned in time to see Cole stride into the kitchen.

"Hey!" Rhonda said, following close on his heels. "Don't you mess with her! You do, and I'll be *all over* you! Do you hear me?"

Ginny stared at him, and her heart nearly stopped. He was even more gorgeous than she remembered, tall and imposing in a leather jacket, jeans and boots.

"I'm not going to mess with her, Rhonda," Cole said evenly.

"Then why are you here? Tell me this minute, 'cause I can dial the sheriff quicker than you can spit."

"Rhonda?" Cole said. "Do you mind leaving us alone for a minute?"

Rhonda glared at him, then shot Ginny a quick look to see if that was okay. Ginny nodded.

"If you need anything, sweetie, you just holler, okay?"

Ginny nodded again, and Rhonda slunk out of the room, giving Cole the evil eye the whole way out. Once she was gone, the room was so quiet Ginny swore she could hear her own heartbeat.

Cole pulled out a chair. "I need to talk to you."

"You've said plenty already."

He closed his eyes. "I know. But please, just listen to me one more time."

She picked up the phone number of the clinic. "Actually, Cole, I was just getting ready to call the clinic. The results of my pregnancy test are in." She took a deep breath, trying to calm her unsteady nerves. "I suppose you need to know, too, and now is as good a time as any."

Cole pulled the piece of paper out of her hand, crumpled it up and tossed it aside.

"What are you doing? You can't hide from this, Cole. We have to know the results!"

"First things first."

He pulled a legal-size document from his coat pocket. "This is your copy of our divorce papers, signed and executed."

He slid the papers in front of her. Tears immediately sprang to her eyes.

No. Stop it. Don't you dare cry.

He'd already done it. He'd already filed the papers. And he was forcing her to wait to find out if she was pregnant until he was quite certain she knew for a fact that they were divorced and she had no hold on him anymore.

She picked up the papers, her hands shaking. Tears blurred

her eyes, and she blinked rapidly to clear them. Finally the words came into focus.

She looked at the document, then looked again. The date. There was something wrong with the date.

"I don't understand," she said, staring at the papers dumbly. "You're a day too early. You were supposed to wait until tomorrow to execute this."

"I know."

"The will was very clear."

"I know that, too."

"If Murphy sees this—"

"Murphy has seen it. I gave him a copy of it myself."

"What did he say?"

"He said I didn't fulfill the provisions of the will."

Ginny stared at him, unable to believe that after all they'd been through so he could get his hands on the deed to the ranch, he'd messed things up so badly at the last minute. And he was acting as if none of it mattered to him in the least.

"Don't you know what you've done?" she said.

"Yeah, Ginny. I know."

He inched closer to her, placing his hand over hers. It was shaking. He started to speak, stopped, bowed his head for a moment and took in a deep, silent breath. When he raised his head again, his eyes were glistening.

"I sure hope you meant it when you said that all you want is me, because as of right now, that's all I have left to give you."

Ginny stared at him, stunned. Little by little, she started to understand, but it was several moments before the full impact of what Cole had done finally hit home. He'd thrown away the ranch in the final hour, stripping himself of everything he thought he ever wanted. And he was coming to her with the only thing he had left to give her.

Himself.

"I said some terrible things to you that day at the ranch," he said. "Words I'd give anything to take back. I know you didn't forget those pills on purpose. I was horrible to you, and you've got every right to tell me to go to hell. But I'm begging you, Ginny." He grasped her hand tightly, then brought it to his lips and kissed it. "Don't leave me. *Please* don't leave me."

His dark eyes shone with tears, and he clenched his jaw to keep them from falling.

"You told me that day that you loved me," he said, his voice a choked whisper. "Did you mean it?"

In his eyes she saw every bit of hurt he'd ever suffered, every moment in his life when he'd loved someone and that love hadn't been returned. And the fact that he'd open his heart enough to ask her that question right now...

But still she was wary. "A lot has happened between us, Cole. I don't know if I can forget that. I don't know—"

"No. Don't say it. Don't say this won't work. Damn it, Ginny, I'll do anything—anything..."

He squeezed his eyes closed, taking a long, shaky breath. "I know that up to now I've acted like we're just friends. That sex between us is just sex. It's not. It hasn't been for a long time now. When I make love to you, that's just what it is. Love."

Ginny put her hand over her mouth, tears filling her eyes. For a moment her throat felt so tight she couldn't speak.

"I love you, Ginny. I've never said that to another human being, not since I was a kid, and I'm not sure I did even then. But I love you. And even if you tell me to go away now, I'll never stop loving you. Never."

He fixed his gaze on hers, a strong, unwavering gaze that told her every word he'd spoken was the truth. But he hadn't just told her. He'd shown her. He'd thrown away the one thing he thought he wanted above all else just to show her he loved her more, to prove to her she was the only thing that would make his life complete.

"I'll never stop loving you, either," she whispered.

He blinked. "Does that mean—"

She slid into his arms, tears cascading down her face. She wound her arms around his neck in a desperate hug. He wrapped his arms around her, pulling her close, whispering against her ear.

"Oh, God. I thought I'd lost you. I thought—" He kissed her temple, her forehead, her lips. "Forgive me, Ginny. I swear I'll never hurt you again."

He hugged her so tightly she could barely breathe, but she didn't care. She wanted to stay in his arms forever.

"But this means we have a problem."

"Problem?"

"We're divorced." He swept her hair from her cheeks and took her face in his hands. "Ginny, will you marry me?"

She remembered the day he'd first said those words to her, how hard they'd been for him to say even when the marriage was going to be nothing but a sham. But now the words flowed from his mouth as if he'd been destined to say them, full of emotion, full of energy.

Full of love.

"Yes," she said, smiling through her tears. "Yes. I'll marry you."

He kissed her, a long, lingering kiss that made her practically melt into the chair. Then she looked at the crumpled phone message.

"Cole, the clinic. We have to know."

"No. Not until after the wedding."

"Why?"

"Because I don't want there ever to be any question in your mind why I married you. I'm not doing it because of a pregnancy. I'm not doing it because I feel responsible for you or any baby you might be carrying. I'm doing it because I love you."

She kissed him, then traced her fingertip along his cheek. "I love you, too."

"So do I get to be the matron of honor?"

They whipped around to see Rhonda standing at the kitchen door.

"Rhonda!" Ginny said. "Were you eavesdropping?"

"Only a little. I'm sorry, Ginny. I just had to make sure what this guy was up to. But, you know, as it turns out, he finally got things right."

"Rhonda?" Cole said. "You think Earl might like to be my best man?"

"Nope. He'd hate it, particularly if you make him wear a tux."

"But he'll do it anyway, won't he?"

"Oh, you bet he will, even if I have to get out the shotgun."

Ginny grinned. "So I suppose you're going to be taking me back to Cupid's Little Chapel of Love."

"Not on your life, sweetheart. Murphy offered us the ranch house. How does that sound?"

Ginny blinked. "What?"

"When I gave him our divorce papers, I told him I was going to do everything I could to get you to marry me again. He expressed extreme doubt that you'd have me, but he said in the event that I got very, very lucky, he'd be willing to host the wedding."

Host the wedding? Murphy?

"He and I will probably never see eye to eye on everything, Ginny, but it's going to be okay now."

Ginny just about started crying again. This day got better and better.

"What's the fastest you can get a wedding together?" Cole asked.

"Well, I don't know," Ginny said, flustered. "If it's a real wedding, we have to have a minister and a cake, and I have to find something to wear— Oh! And invitations! Of course, I'd like to invite a few people—"

"One week," Rhonda said.

"One week it is," Cole said.

One week. That was fast. Way too fast. But then again, the quicker they were married, the quicker Cole would be hers forever.

And in the end, that was all she'd ever wanted.

Later, at home, Ginny pulled from her pocket the crumpled piece of paper that held the phone number of the clinic. Cole had said it didn't matter, but still she was worried.

"Cole? What if I really am pregnant? Are you really all right with it? However it turns out?"

Cole took her hand. "If it happens that we get that little wedding present, I'll be the happiest man alive. And if it turns out that we don't..." He brought her hand to his lips and kissed it. "I'll still be the happiest man alive."

"Then let's find out."

Cole smiled and nodded, and Ginny picked up the telephone.

Epilogue

ONE WEEK LATER, Ginny and Cole stood on the veranda of the ranch house, staring at the rolling hills, beautiful even in the starkness of near-winter. The usual cold of early December had forced them to plan an indoor wedding, but to their surprise, the afternoon sun shone so brightly on the veranda that the temperature shot up to an unseasonably warm level for Texas, and they moved the ceremony outdoors.

Cole couldn't believe how beautiful Ginny looked. Her dress was simple but elegant, tucked at the waist and falling in soft folds to her ankles, with a neckline that dipped just low enough to be a little bit daring. Sweet and sexy at the same time.

Just like Ginny.

He'd worn a tuxedo for the occasion because he'd wanted to do this right, even though he longed for jeans and boots. He wasn't doing nearly as much longing as Earl was, though. Fortunately, Rhonda kept him in line with an occasional swat on the arm when he fiddled too much with his tie. Loretta and Darlene came, too, as well as Ruby and most of the people from the bank.

Pastor McDonald from the First Baptist Church of Coldwater performed the ceremony, which was a whole lot more traditional than the one they'd had at Cupid's Little Chapel of Love. They swore him to silence about the real nature of their marriage, because for all anyone except Rhonda, Earl and Murphy knew, they were merely renewing their wedding vows with a more formal ceremony among friends after six blissful months of marriage.

After a short ceremony, complete with a new ring for Ginny, they both said their I do's and Cole kissed the bride. He needed no persuasion this time except to *stop* kissing her, which he finally did after extensive throat-clearing from Pastor McDonald.

Afterward, while Ginny was chatting with their guests, Cole stepped to the railing of the veranda and looked out over the acres of pastureland. For all his protest about hating this place, he knew now how much he was going to miss it.

Murphy came up beside him. "You're a lucky man. But then, surely I don't have to tell you that."

"No, Murphy. You don't."

"I think maybe I was wrong about a few things."

"I think maybe you weren't."

Murphy looked at him with surprise.

"I never meant to hurt my grandmother. I know I didn't come back when I should have, and—"

"It's over. Forget about it."

"I loved her, Murphy."

Murphy got a faraway look in his eyes. "So did I, Cole."

As Cole looked at Murphy, it was as if a shroud slowly fell away and he saw him clearly for the very first time. Memories came flooding back of Murphy and his grandmother, of them laughing, embracing and even kissing when they didn't know he was watching. He remembered sitting at the kitchen table in the mornings and seeing Murphy come down the back stairs. His grandmother's face would light up with love, and Murphy would give her a smile in return that said he loved her, too.

Until recently he'd thought of Murphy as nothing but an angry old man. So why did all these other memories come back only now? Where had they been buried all these years?

In a rush of understanding, he knew it wasn't that Murphy had hated him. It was that he'd loved Edna, so much so he'd go to war with anyone who tried to hurt her. Her death had only intensified that loyalty. He'd been forced both to carry out her wishes and protect her memory, doing everything he could to insure the woman he loved would never be hurt by Cole or anyone else, whether she was in this world or the next.

Now, finally, because of Ginny, Cole understood that kind of love.

Murphy nodded toward Ginny. "What made you finally wise up?"

Cole turned to look at his wife, catching her eye. She smiled, a warm, wonderful smile that was meant only for him.

"It's the way she looks at me," he said.

Murphy turned and looked at him, his blue eyes sharp as ever.

"See, Murphy, some men wait their whole lives for a woman to look at them like that. I figured I'd better not let her get away."

Murphy nodded. "Smart man."

"It reminds me of the way my grandmother looked at you."

Murphy's eyes got a little misty. "Not a day goes by that I don't think about her."

"Maybe we're both smart men."

"Maybe we are."

In that moment, Cole felt the ten years he'd spent so full of anger and resentment slip away like a bad dream at daybreak.

"Why don't you ask your wife to come over here for a minute?"

Cole wondered what was up. He did as Murphy asked and

called to Ginny. She left the guests and came over, sliding int‹
his arms as naturally as if she'd spent a lifetime doing it.

Murphy reached inside his coat pocket, pulled out an en›
velope and handed it to Cole. Cole opened it, and when h‹
saw what it contained, he was filled with disbelief.

The title to the ranch. In both his name and Ginny's.

Ginny blinked with surprise. "For us?"

Murphy nodded.

She turned to Cole with a questioning look. He knew wha‹
she was wondering, and he didn't blame her. She was wait‹
ing for him to get that look in his eyes again that said he saw
dollar signs.

"Ginny?" he said.

"Yes?"

"Do you want—"

"Do I want what?"

Silence.

"The ranch," Cole said. "I was wondering—"

"What?"

"Ginny? Would you like to stay here?"

She looked at him with astonishment. "Here? On th‹
ranch?"

"Yes."

"You mean we can keep it? We can actually live here?"

"Only if you want to."

"Oh, yes!" She threw her arms around him, practicall‹
squeezing the breath out of him. "Yes!"

"Now, I know you wanted to go to college—"

"But I have my new job. I'm learning so much that I don‹
want to stop now. Maybe I'll go to college later, but fo‹
now—" she kissed Cole "—this is where I want to stay."

Then she turned to Murphy. She wrapped her arms aroun‹
his neck and kissed him on the cheek, then whispered som‹

thing in his ear. Murphy smiled a little and whispered something back.

Cole watched Murphy walk away. "So what did you say to him?"

"That's none of your business."

"Sure it is," he said with a smile. "We're married now. For real. Everything's my business."

Ginny's eyes filled with tears. "I said, 'I told you so.'"

Cole realized just how much Ginny had believed in him all this time, even when he'd done nothing to deserve it, and for a moment he was sick with the feeling of how close he'd come to losing her. He'd never make that kind of mistake again.

"And what did Murphy say to you?"

"He said you're just the kind of man your grandmother always believed you could be."

Cole's throat felt so tight he couldn't speak. At the same time, though, a peaceful feeling settled over him, a feeling that he'd finally come home where he belonged.

Ginny turned and looked out over the ranch. "It's beautiful, isn't it?"

"Yes," Cole said. "I can't think of a better place to raise our baby."

He pulled Ginny close, enveloping her in his arms. They'd tell everyone else soon enough. But for right now, it was a secret only they shared.

Cole encouraged their guests to stay the rest of the afternoon and into the evening, basking in the feeling of being surrounded by friends and, in the case of Murphy, family. As much as he wanted to be alone with his wife, for once he was in no hurry.

After all, he and Ginny would be together for the rest of their lives.

*H*ugh Blake,
soon to become stepfather to
the Maitland clan, has produced three
high-performing offspring of his own. But
at the rate they're going, they're never going to
make him a grandpa!

There's *Suzanne*, a work-obsessed CEO whose Christmas spirit
could use a little topping up....

And *Thomas*, a lawyer whose ability to hold on to the woman
he loves is evaporating by the minute....

And *Diane*, a teacher so dedicated to her teenage students she
hasn't noticed she's put her own life on hold.

But there's a Christmas wake-up call in store
for the Blake siblings. Love *and* Christmas miracles
are in store for all three!

Maitland Maternity Christmas

A collection from three of Harlequin's favorite authors

Muriel Jensen
Judy Christenberry
&Tina Leonard

Look for it in November 2001.

Look to the stars
for love and romance
with bestselling authors

JUDITH ARNOLD
KATE HOFFMANN
and GINA WILKINS

in

WRITTEN
IN THE
STARS

Experience the joy of
three women who dare to
make their wishes for love
and happiness come true in
this *brand-new* collection
from Harlequin!

Available in December 2001
at your favorite retail outlet.

HARLEQUIN®
Makes any time special ®

ADDED BONUS:
As a special gift to our readers, a 30-page 2002
Love Guide will be included in this collection!

*Together for the first time
in one Collector's Edition!*

New York Times bestselling authors

Barbara Delinsky

Catherine Coulter Linda Howard

Forever Yours

**A special trade-size volume containing three
complete novels that showcase the passion,
imagination and stunning power that these
talented authors are famous for.**

Coming to your favorite retail outlet in December 2001.

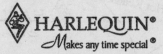

HARLEQUIN®
Makes any time special ®